SABRE PILOT

SABRE PILOT

STEPHEN W. MEADER

Illustrated by John Polgreen

ISBN 978-1-931177-14-6 cloth
ISBN 978-1-931177-15-3 paperback

SOUTHERN SKIES

LITTLE ROCK, ARKANSAS
www.southernskies.com

Dedication

The republication of this book is dedicated with gratitude and affection to Joanne Scott by her friend and partner, Jerry Atchley.

More than a dozen years ago my two sons, both pilots in what was then the Army Air Corps, asked me why I didn't write a story about flying. From their experiences I could have drawn plenty of background for such a book. Also, during World War II, I was deeply involved with military aviation —writing advertising for Boeing and for Air Corps Recruiting. Yet I hesitated for one reason. I was not a pilot myself, and the skill and courage of the youngsters who were building our air power made me feel humble.

When a pair of persuasive Air Force captains visited me a year ago and asked me to do a book about a young jet fighter pilot, my first inclination was to refuse again. But as they outlined the possibilities and showed me stark, unvarnished accounts of combat, capture, and escape never before seen by civilian eyes, I began to weaken. Finally they offered the full facilities of the Air Force for research trips to various training bases, and I agreed to tackle the job.

Now that *Sabre Pilot* is finished, I realize that only a man who has trained, lived, and fought as a jet jockey could do full justice to the subject. As it is, I offer no apologies. I have tried to put into this story some of the boundless respect and admiration I feel for the Air Force. If it helps to inspire even a few of my readers to choose careers in the air, I shall be satisfied.

A complete list of the officers and airmen who helped make the book possible would fill several pages. I would like especially to express my gratitude to Captains James Sunderman and Phil Garrison, of the Office of Information Services, Department of the Air Force; and to my son John, who worked fully as hard as I at gathering material and keeping the flight on course.

STEPHEN W. MEADER

April, 1956

SABRE PILOT

The June night lay hot and quiet over the countryside. Along the back roads where the three small cars were moving, there was no other traffic, no lights in the farmhouses. Late as it was, the moonrise was still only a pale blur in the east.

Kirk Owen, in the last of the three cars, listened contentedly to the purr of his engine. It was tuned right, and the warm, damp air of the night seemed to agree with its digestion. Up ahead he could see Joe Flack making the turn in his cut-down Ford. The MG, with Gary Kelso at the wheel, was cornering neatly behind it. Three or four more miles and they'd be at the old airfield.

Kirk's own machine was a sort of mongrel, called, for want of a better name, the Owen Special. He had built it himself out of the remains of two wrecked Austin A-40's. The engine came from one, the frame, wheels, and brakes from the other. The steering rack and pinion were off a junked MG-TD. And the body was lifted from an old midget racer, split down the middle and widened with an aluminum strip that ran from the oval radiator scoop clear back to the tail. Its lines were low and racy in spite of the headlights mounted on brackets on either side of the hood. It even looked, he flattered himself, a little like a J-2 Allard.

Off and on, Kirk had given a great many hours of loving care to the little bug. Not even going off to college had stopped him. Prowling the junk yards in the university town, he had been able to pick up a Stromberg 97 two-barrel carburetor and a Ford transverse spring, which had to be shortened and reworked to fit the narrower tread.

Meanwhile, in week ends and vacations at home, he had bored out sixteen holes in each of the four disc wheels to lighten and cool them. He still groaned when he remembered the long, blistery job of cutting those holes with a circular hacksaw blade mounted on his old hand drill.

A new head had given the engine more compression, and he had reamed the ports for bigger valves. He had weighed and balanced the pistons and polished the intake manifold to gleaming smoothness. What he had, at last, could hardly be called a hot rod. It was more of a sports job. He knew it wouldn't win many drag races, but on the open road he figured he ought to get a top speed of at least a hundred miles an hour. And the gas mileage should make it an economical car to drive.

A waning half-moon was creeping above the trees when they reached the high wire fence along the side of the field. Joe drove slowly, looking for landmarks.

"There it is," he called back in a low voice. "There by the busted fence-post."

He stopped the Ford and went over to the fence. After a moment's work with a pair of pliers he pulled away a section of the rusted wire, folding it back to leave a seven-foot opening. Then, as he was about to get into the car, they saw him stop, staring at the wide, flat field beyond.

"Funny," he said. "You guys notice anything different?"

"Sure," Gary answered. "The grass an' weeds have been cut. A good thing, too—they were high as your waist, some places."

"Come on," Kirk called impatiently. "Let's go in. Some farmer probably mowed it for hay—that's all."

One by one the little cars jolted across the shallow ditch and through the gap in the fence. For a hundred yards the stubble swished beneath their tires. Then they were out on a broad concrete landing strip.

Jennison Field had been rushed to completion back in wartime. It was built to handle the big four-engine bombers —B-17's, B-24's and B-29's—on their training flights. Now only two or three ramshackle hangars and a frame control tower remained at the end of the field near the gate. It was just another abandoned air base, too far from any large city for any commercial use. Occasionally a small plane landed there in an emergency, but there were no lights or radio facilities, and the tower was never manned.

As far as the boys were concerned, the forgotten field served just one useful purpose. Its 8000-foot runways were an ideal place to test the speed of a car with no danger of breaking any highway traffic laws.

Slowly they drove to the south end of the strip. Another runway intersected it there, making an angle like the blades of a pair of scissors. Up at the far end they knew a third, shorter strip cut across both, forming the base of a triangle.

They lined up, with the engines running.

"What you want to try first?" asked Joe, the garage mechanic. "Me—I'd like to take you guys on an' show you what real acceleration looks like."

Gary Kelso grinned. "All right," he said. "Might as well get it over. We know you've got a lot of sting in that bomb, but you won't be happy till you've proved it. I'll give the signal to start."

Slowly he counted up to three and yelled "Go!"

Kirk had been revving up gently in neutral. He whipped the lever into low gear, shifting up as the little car shot ahead. For the first half mile he held the MG fairly even. Then he began to pull ahead. But at the end of the roughly measured mile, marked by a striped wind vane in the infield, the hopped-up Ford was leading them both by a good three hundred yards.

"Wow!" Joe Flack was chortling when they hauled up beside him. "The old rod's really windin' up tonight! Know how long it took me to hit sixty? Under nine seconds!"

"Nice going," Kirk agreed. "Now how about a couple of laps around the triangle—say six miles or so?"

"That's more like it," said Gary with a satisfied nod. "Let's find out who's got the real road car."

They turned around and lined up again opposite the wind tee. Joe called the signal this time. As before, he led by a considerable margin after the take-off, but he lost most of the advantage when he slowed down for the first sharp corner. Kirk took a firm grip on the wheel and went into the tight turn at fifty. Right on his heels came the little British sports car, while Joe Flack went squealing and side-slipping to the outer edge of the concrete.

The low-slung Owen Special came out of the bend without a sign of a skid, all four tires holding the road. Kirk felt a tingle of reckless joy run down his spine. He drew a deep exultant breath and gunned the engine in a fresh surge of speed.

He was still holding the lead at the upper turn, pulling away from the MG little by little. And Joe's hot rod had dropped out of competition after skidding onto the grass and nearly rolling over. Kirk took the final corner of the three-legged course and roared down the straightaway once more. Then, right in his path, he saw the sudden glare of headlights.

The boy reacted fast. All in one instant he pulled to the right, not too hard, lifted his foot from the accelerator, and began pumping the brake pedal. Luckily the strip was wide enough to give him room. He had been hitting eighty. As he flashed past the other car, he had already begun to slow down, but he didn't dare steal a glance from his driving to see who the newcomer was. Behind him he could hear a scream of brakes from the MG.

Kirk stopped, a hundred yards down the runway, and looked over his shoulder. Gary pulled up beside him.

"Who the devil was that?" his friend growled. "Might have killed us both!"

They turned their cars cautiously and cruised back up the strip. Sitting there waiting for them was a jeep. The man in it got out and held up his hand as they approached. Kirk had expected a state policeman, but this fellow wore light tan trousers and blouse. A blue uniform cap was pushed back on his head, and on his arm band were the big letters A.P. The other sleeve bore sergeant's stripes. He strolled over to the Owen Special.

"You boys know you're trespassing on government property?" he asked. There was no gruffness in his tone, but one look at his square-jawed, weather-browned face told Kirk he was nobody to be trifled with.

"Sorry," he answered. "I guess we thought the government wasn't interested in it any more. Nobody's been here for years."

"Must be you don't read the papers," the sergeant said. "This field was reactivated last week. Using the runways for a race track is bad enough, but cutting the fence means you're in real trouble."

"That place in the fence has been broken for more'n a year," Gary put in. "And we didn't cut it. All we do is pull back the wire when we want to come in, and we always hook it up again."

They were all three standing in the illumination of the headlights now. The sergeant turned and looked Gary over, much as he had sized up Kirk. Before he spoke, the deep bass rumble of the Ford's straight pipe exhaust came nearer, and Joe pulled into the circle of light.

"What's up?" he asked. "Oh-oh—Air Police, huh?" The sergeant eyed him with a wintry smile. "That's right," he said. "And just so there'll be no misunderstanding, I'll repeat what I already told this lad here. The Air Force is reactivating Jennison AFB. I got out here yesterday and had the grass cut. A company of engineers'll be here tomorrow to check on the concrete, start some new buildings, an' maybe lengthen the runways. Inside of a month there'll be planes based here."

He paused, frowning. "I could take the three of you in for trespass," he continued at last. "But I don't think I will. You've done no damage that I can see. On the other hand, I'm afraid I can't let you finish your race. Guess I'd look sort of silly if I stood here watching and the colonel happened to drop by.

"Matter o' fact," he added with a grin, "I don't blame you for coming out here. It's about the only place where you can let a car really roll without being a danger to anybody but yourselves. You know we've got a couple o' generals in the Air Force that like fast cars, too. I've seen 'em working out on the runways down in Florida."

His easy manner had won them over. "You been in the Air Force long?" Joe Flack asked him.

"Ten years," he said. "Since before Pearl Harbor. Done everything from repairing engines in Burma to flying tailgunner in a B-24. The Air Police business is just peacetime duty. But with this week's news out o' Korea, maybe peacetime is over. By the way, how do you fellows stand in the draft?"

"I've done my service," Joe replied promptly. "Two years in the motor pool at Fort Dix. Now I'm chief mechanic in a garage."

"Navy for me," Gary told him. "I'm going in next week, so I guess this is about my last time out with the MG."

The sergeant nodded, then turned to Kirk. "How about you, son?" he said.

"I'll probably be called pretty soon," the boy answered. "Had a college deferment, but I dropped out when Dad had a heart attack last April."

"College, eh? You don't look more than seventeen."

"I'll be eighteen in August," Kirk replied a bit stiffly. "I was sixteen when I entered State U."

"Must have been a pretty smart lad," said the airman. "Nearly two years of college—wish I'd had the same."

He moved over to the little Owen Special. "It looked to me as if you had that race in the bag," he chuckled. "Too bad I had to stop it, but you were really pouring it on 'em. What you got under that hood, anyhow?"

Kirk showed him. As he talked, the boy's reserve fell away, for he had an understanding audience. The veteran airman really knew something about engines.

"Tell you what," the sergeant said at length. "It's time you fellows got out o' here. I wasn't kidding about the colonel coming around. He's liable to wake up at three in the morning and get an idea he wants to look at the base. But I'd like to come around to your place tomorrow if you're going to be home. I'll bring some tools. Maybe we can get a little more out o' that little mill of yours. How do I get to your place?"

Kirk gave him the address. "Maybe you'd better make it in the evening," he said. "I've got some lawns to cut tomorrow. Doing odd jobs is the only work I could get, but it helps out until Dad's able to go back to the office. Why don't you come to supper? My folks would like to meet you."

The sergeant laughed. "It sounds good," he replied, "but

I reckon an invitation like that had better come from your mother. I'll be 'round there about seven."

He got back into the jeep and drove to the main gate with the three cars following him. There he bade them a pleasant good night and watched them take off down the road.

Kirk saw Joe and Gary ahead of him hitting it up on a straight stretch. Their taillights slipped out of sight over a rise, and he made no effort to chase them. At the moment he wanted to think. This sergeant—he realized he didn't even know his name—was a pretty nice sort of guy. He seemed to like his job, too. There was pride in the way he wore his trim-fitting uniform and authority in his quiet voice. If he came to the house tomorrow night, Kirk had a hunch there would be more talk about the Air Force. Those questions about their draft status—they had been leading up to something. Well, he asked himself, why not? There were a lot worse ways for a youngster to spend his military service than in the Air Force. Maybe he'd even get a chance to work on engines—jet engines. A tingle ran down his spine as he parked the little car under a shed in the back yard and tiptoed up to bed.

2

Clarksdale, where Kirk lived, was a town of ten or twelve thousand people in the heart of the Corn Belt. A lot of prosperous farmers did their shopping there, and there were two or three small industries that gave employment to some of the townspeople. Mr. Owen had been assistant manager at the overall factory, and his job was still open when he was well enough to return.

Kirk had one sister, Margie, a youngster of twelve, who

would be starting high school in the fall. She was a light sleeper. Before the boy could reach his room, her door opened down the hall.

"Hey," she whispered, "how'd it go? Did you beat 'em?"

"I don't know," he told her. "I was ahead, but we had to call it off. They're opening up the field again. Look, you little pest—what are you doing up this time of night. Must be after one o'clock."

"I heard your car come in. What do you mean—did somebody stop you?"

"Yes. The Air Police. Lucky they didn't stick us in jail. Now go to bed before you wake Mother up."

It was hot in his room. He stripped and lay on the bed without even a sheet over him, and it was some time before he got to sleep. As a consequence he didn't wake up until nearly nine, with a high sun blazing into his eyes.

Mrs. Owen was in the kitchen and set about getting his breakfast when he came down.

"What kind of a night did Dad have?" he asked. "Pretty hot to sleep, wasn't it?"

"He did pretty well," she answered. "Hot weather never bothers him much, and he's really better these days. You were out a bit late yourself, weren't you, son? Margie said you got in a little trouble at the airfield."

"Well," he told her, "not real trouble. A nice, friendly guy from the Air Force was there, and he stopped us from driving on the runways. Said they were starting to reactivate the base. He's coming around here tonight to help me work on the car."

"That's nice," she said. "Did you invite him to supper?"

"I tried to, but he just laughed. Said he couldn't do that without a bid from you."

She smiled. "Sounds as if he had more sense than some men I've known," she said.

Kirk oiled up the mower and set off to cut his lawns. Wearing nothing but blue jeans and sneakers, he let the sun beat on his already tanned back and chest. By four that afternoon he had made five dollars and lost several pounds. He came home, took a shower, and found a big pitcher of lemonade waiting for him when he came downstairs.

His father was sitting on the screened porch, where shade and a little breeze made it comfortable. Kirk took his drink out there and lolled back luxuriously on the glider.

"Sort of hot work today, wasn't it?" Mr. Owen remarked. "Careful you don't get sunstroke."

The boy grinned and stretched his wiry brown arms. "Not me," he said. "Any kid raised in this part o' the country is used to hot weather, I guess. Anyhow, I was able to give Mother five bucks toward the housekeeping money."

His father's face was grave. "Thanks," he said. "Sorry you couldn't get a regular summer job, but I know it's tough when the draft board may call you any time. Give me another few weeks of rest and I'll be able to go back to the plant."

"Gosh, Dad, don't rush it," Kirk told him. "We're doing okay." He changed the subject. "There's an Air Force sergeant coming to see me tonight. I want you to meet him."

The airman was as good as his word. Hardly had the supper dishes been washed and put away when he drove his jeep up to the door. This time he was in fatigues and wearing the long-billed baseball cap of an air mechanic. He took a battered toolbox out of the car and hailed Kirk cheerfully.

"Where's that little boiler of yours?" he asked. "The way she was running last night I doubt if I can make any improvements, but I like to fool with 'em anyway."

They rolled the Special out of the shed and took off the hood. For an hour they tinkered and tested, tried a richer

mixture, then leaned it down till they assured themselves the carburetor was set exactly right.

"You've got a sweet little job there," said the sergeant at last, mopping his face. "What kind of mileage do you get in ordinary driving?"

"Around thirty-five miles to the gallon. I guess the engine would have given me forty or better before it was souped up. Why don't you come in an' meet my folks? I'll show you where to wash up if you'd like. And by the way, I never got your name."

"That's right," the older man chuckled. "I'm Ivar Nelson. And I'll take you up on that wash."

They took showers, dressed again, and came down to find all the Owens enjoying the cool dusk on the porch.

"Mother and Dad," said Kirk with some formality, "I'd like you to meet Staff Sergeant Ivar Nelson, U.S. Air Force. Sergeant, Mr. and Mrs. Owen—and this sprout is my kid sister, Margie."

Nelson shook hands politely all around and took the edge

off Kirk's introduction by showing special courtesy to the young lady of the household.

"Are you a career man in the Air Force?" Mr. Owen asked when they were all seated.

"I guess you'd call it that," the sergeant replied. "Ten years, and I still like it fine. I'm in the Air Police right now, but that's just temporary duty, I hope."

"I suppose you get shifted around a lot," Mrs. Owen put in. "Isn't that hard on your family—or don't you have one?"

"Yes, I do, Ma'am—a wife and two boys—four and three. They don't seem to mind it. You see, we've got a nice little house on the Post. When I move out, they go with me, like the three years I spent in Japan after the war. It's a pretty good life."

In response to their questioning, he told a few of his war experiences briefly and with due modesty. On the subject of his family he was more expansive.

"My wife and I are both from Wisconsin," he explained. "I'd been writing to her all through the war, and when I got a long leave, after the Japs surrendered, I came home an' married her in Green Bay. We make enough to live on, and in ten more years I can retire with half pay. I went in when I was eighteen, so I'll only be thirty-eight. What's more, I've learned a skilled trade in the Air Force, and I reckon I'll be able to get a pretty good job—maybe in an aircraft plant."

Quiet until now, Kirk wondered if this was the time to speak. There was a pause in the conversation, and his voice sounded louder than he had intended.

"Dad," he said, "I'd like to go in the Air Force myself.

"You see," he hurried on, "if I enlisted now, I'd have my choice of services. Another few weeks and it might be too late—I'd be called up and sent wherever they wanted."

"Well," his father hesitated, "I was hoping you could go back to college in September if you could make up the work you lost this spring. Maybe the draft board would change their rules."

"I doubt it," said Kirk. "With this Korean thing, they've had to push up their quotas." He turned to Sergeant Nelson. "Think they'd take me in the Air Force?"

The airman looked pleased. "I'm sure of it," he answered. "If your father agreed, that is. You're still under eighteen you told me."

He looked toward Mr. Owen. "You know, sir," he said, "the boy's got real mechanical ability. I admit, if he could have gone on in school, he might have gotten an engineering degree. But it won't be too late for that after he's done his service. Meanwhile, everything he learns in the Air Force will help. And he's needed now. There'll be a lot of airplanes to keep in shape before this is over."

The last argument seemed to weigh with Mr. Owen. He regarded his son thoughtfully for a moment, then turned to his wife with a smile.

"What do you say, Mary? You ready to let him go?"

Kirk's mother surprised him. "Yes," she said without hesitation. "He's going to be called anyway, and this is what he wants. I guess no mother likes to see her son go into uniform, but there's a lot in what the sergeant says. Kirk, why don't you run down to the corner and get a quart of ice cream? We might as well celebrate."

The boy needed no urging. His heart was high as he filled the plates for Margie to serve. It was all he could do to keep from humming the tune about the "wild blue yonder." Then he remembered that anything he did in the Air Force would probably be strictly on the ground and restrained himself.

It was agreed, before the sergeant left, that Kirk would

be at the post office next morning as soon as the recruiting booth opened. Nelson promised to come, too, if he could make it. "But you won't have any trouble," he said. "Young Brodie'll be on duty, and he knows me. Mention my name if you like."

For the second night in a row it took Kirk a long time to get to sleep. The thrill of his decision was tempered somewhat, now that he got to thinking about it. How would they receive him at the recruiting station? Would the draft board upset his plans? And, if the Air Force did accept him, what would it be like going off to some distant camp with a bunch of total strangers? This would be different from entering college. He'd be in a wholly new world.

Finally he laughed at himself. What was he anyhow—a baby? He rolled over on his side and went to sleep.

Promptly at nine o'clock the next morning he set out for the post office. He had put on his good slacks and shoes and a new T-shirt. His wavy, brown hair was slicked back neatly. And he carried a note, signed by his father, that he had his parents' permission to enlist.

The whole procedure was easier than he expected. Young Sergeant Brodie was in the booth, and he seemed to be expecting the boy.

"Let's see," he said. "Kirk Owen, eh? And you want to join the Air Force? All right, sit over there and fill in this form. Here's a pen."

The questions were simple enough. They dealt with such matters as age, place of birth, education, and criminal record, if any.

"I see you're under eighteen," said the sergeant when Kirk returned the paper. "Your father'll have to sign the application. Can he come down here?"

"He's resting up from a heart attack," Kirk told him. "He really shouldn't come out in this heat."

"That's all right; your mother'll do. Or better yet, I'll go to the house with you. First, though, I'll call up the draft board and make sure you're in the clear."

The telephone line was busy. Brodie turned the booth over to his helper, a Marine PFC, and he and Kirk went down the street together to the Selective Service office. The secretary checked the files for Kirk's record.

"Well," he said, "we had this young man on the list for next month's quota, but if he wants to join the Air Force, more power to him. Let me know as soon as he's accepted, and I'll make the entry on his file."

Half an hour later, with the form duly signed by Mr. Owen, they returned to the recruiting station. Sergeant Nelson was waiting for them there. He grinned at Kirk and gave him a hard, brown hand.

"I guess you're in, son," he said. "Right, Brodie? All that's left is the official ceremony."

In the quiet of the postmaster's private office, Kirk took the oath of allegiance. He stood facing the American flag, with the two sergeants flanking him. As he repeated the solemn words, there was a choke in his voice. Unconsciously he squared his shoulders. He had taken on a new responsibility.

When it was over, they all shook hands again. "Pretty soon," Brodie chuckled, "you won't be palling around with sergeants. You'll be saluting 'em—and probably hating their guts! You are now the lowest form of animal life—a recruit in the U.S. Air Force."

"But not for long," Nelson assured him. "This boy's got the makings of a good airman. Where'll he be sent? Lackland?"

"That's right," said Brodie. "I've got two more headed that way. There'll be a train through here from Chicago with a special car Monday morning. They ought to be in San Antone by the next night."

Kirk's head was in a whirl as he walked home. He'd heard of Lackland Air Force Base. One of the biggest and finest in the country. And San Antonio, Texas! The name had a romantic sound to a small-town boy who had never been out of his own state. It suggested cowboy boots and spurs and ten-gallon hats—the Alamo and Davy Crockett.

He had two days to get ready. First he had to tell his friends, Joe Flack and Gary Kelso. Joe, with his Army service behind him, was inclined to laugh at his enthusiasm.

"Sure," he said. "You'll feel like a sucker an' you'll just have to sweat it out. You'll hate the lousy chow an' all the rest of it. You'll find some good guys and some stinkers, but you'll be wishing it was over from the time you get in. It's just one o' those things a kid has to take these days."

Gary was more impressed. "You ought to have some fun down in Texas," he said. "I guess I'll be at Great Lakes, an' they say Chicago's a good town for shore leave. Maybe I'll see you if we both get leaves at the same time. You better send me a card so I'll know your address, an' I'll try to write you."

Kirk's mother was anxious that he should have everything he needed. He had to laugh her out of ironing all his shirts and pressing his best suit.

"Look, Mom," he said, "you just keep these things here for me. All I'm taking is a toothbrush and shaving kit, a pair of pajamas and a clean T-shirt. They'll give me all my clothes, you know."

He mowed half a dozen more lawns, and his father insisted he keep the six dollars for spending money on the trip. One of the hardest things he had to do was bid farewell to his little car. He greased it with care, jacked it up on blocks of wood, and tied an old tarpaulin over it to keep out dust and rain.

Then, almost before he knew it, it was Monday morning. A cool front had moved in during the night, breaking the heat wave. The sky was gray, with a threat of rain, and a wind blew chilly from the north as he stood with his family on the station platform.

The train pulled in on time. Brodie had come down to see his charges safely aboard.

"You're down this way," he told Kirk. "Next to the last car. Better hustle."

Mr. Owen shook the boy's hand with a firm grip and a smile. Kirk's mother wept a little, and Margie threw her arms around her brother's neck.

"Good-by, folks," he managed to say. "I'll write. Take care of yourself, Dad."

Then he was off at a lope, heading for the rear of the train.

3

Joe Flack had warned him about that train. "Special car, eh?" he had laughed. "You'll find it's a fifty-year-old wooden day coach most likely—with busted seats as hard as a rock. Nobody can sleep on those things unless they've been hit over the head."

But the car, when he reached it, looked like an ordinary Pullman. He hustled up the steps with his little bag. In the vestibule was a flustered young Air Force lieutenant with a clip-board in his hand.

"Hold it," he ordered sharply. "Let's see your travel

orders. Hm, Owen, Kirk—is that right? Yep—Owen, Gamble, and Canuso. That's the Clarksdale contingent."

He led the way into the car. "We're pretty well filled up," he said. "Guess you'll have to take an upper. Here's one—number eleven."

The seat that faced forward was already occupied by a blond youngster in a loud sport shirt who lay back snoozing, dead to the world. Kirk slipped his bag under the other seat and sat down gingerly on the cushions. To his surprise it was soft and comfortable. He wished Joe Flack could see this luxury.

It was the first time he had ever traveled in a sleeper, and he was full of curiosity. He sat still till the train started, then got up to do some exploring. First of all he located the washroom and smoking compartment, where half a dozen fellows about his own age were lolling on the side benches, getting acquainted.

Then he went through the car looking for the other two lads from Clarksdale. The name Canuso had sounded famil-

iar. Down near the opposite end he found them sitting together in the space marked "three."

"Hi, Tony," he said, and slid in beside the black-haired
Italian boy.

"Kirk Owen, by golly!" Tony exclaimed. "You in the
Air Force? That's swell! I guess you don't know Elmer
Gamble. He's from up the other end o' the county."

Kirk shook hands. Gamble was a big, strapping boy in
jeans and heavy work shoes. He had "farmer" written all
over him, from his huge calloused hands to the faint aroma
of the cow barn that surrounded him. Kirk liked his friendly
grin.

Tony Canuso had been a class behind Kirk in high school.
He was a quick, well-co-ordinated chap who had been something of a star on the baseball and basketball teams.

"What you been doing lately?" Kirk asked him.

"Workin' around my dad's fruit store an' drivin' the
truck," Tony replied. "How come you enlisted? I thought
you were up at State U."

21

Kirk explained why he had had to quit in April. "I figure maybe I can finish college after my hitch," he said. "I was going to be called anyway, so I picked the Air Force."

"Same here," Tony said. "From all I hear it's the best deal in the services. Elmer here, he's different. He could have got deferred, workin' on the farm."

Gamble smiled. "I just don't like the way those Reds are movin' in on the South Koreans," he mumbled. "Thought maybe I ought to do somethin' about it."

"That's right," Tony nodded. "Me, I'd like to get over there. Think we will?"

"Not for a while," said Kirk. "This basic training takes two or three months, and then there's a lot more time in A & E School. The whole Korean thing may be over before we're ready to do much good."

At eleven-thirty the lieutenant moved through the car passing out slips of paper. "The diner's three cars ahead," he told them. "We eat early, before the regular passengers. You'll line up and march through when I give the word."

Five minutes later the twenty-seven recruits were at tables in the dining car. There were no menus for them, and they were all served the same meal—beef stew with vegetables, bread and butter, coffee and apple pie. It was good, plain fare, which most of them ate with enjoyment. They were through in twenty minutes, handing their slips to the steward as they left the diner. Passengers, waiting to get in for lunch, eyed them curiously as they returned in a straggling line to their own car.

They were fed again at five-thirty, after an afternoon spent reading, napping, playing gin rummy, or just talking. By that time Kirk knew most of his companions by name. They were of all kinds—some apparently from well-to-do families, others from the big city slums—some with good educations, others who had quit school after the eighth grade and had to move their lips to read even a comic book. There were two Negroes in the group. One was a very shy, retiring youth. The other was a husky six-footer who had played football on a Chicago high school team. His big laugh and happy-go-lucky ability to tell stories had them all in a good humor.

The discouraged-looking porter came in at nine and made up the berths. He knew there wouldn't be much in the line of tips from this gang. As soon as his upper was ready, Kirk scrambled up and went to bed. The boy in lower eleven was nowhere in sight. He had sneaked out of the line after supper and disappeared forward, in the direction of the club car.

Sometime later Kirk woke to the jolt of couplings. The train had stopped in a big city yard, and more cars were being added. When he got up a little before six, he heard that a lot of new recruits had joined them in the night—two full Pullman loads. Breakfast for the Lackland-bound youngsters had to be served in two shifts, and they were all out of the dining car by seven.

That was a long day. The heat outside grew more intense as they dragged across Oklahoma and into northern Texas. Even in the air-conditioned sleeper the temperature climbed, and the boys were listless. Kirk watched the landscape crawl by—the white glare of sagebrush and sand, the scattered farms and distant oil derricks. Once they stopped at a little town where he saw a pair of dusty cowhands herding a few tired-looking steers into a shipping corral beside the tracks.

Later, when he was sitting with his Clarksdale friends, the country began changing. The ranch houses looked bigger and better kept. Off on the skyline they could see range cattle moving. But there was little to relieve the monotony of browns and grays across the landscape.

"Don't believe I'd like farming here," said Elmer. "Not

enough green stuff growing. I'd rather work with corn an' hogs."

"How are you an' that yellow-haired Chicago kid gettin' along?" Tony asked Kirk. "The one in lower eleven?"

"We don't have much to say. He's got his nose in the air —acts as if he didn't want to associate with the rest of us any more'n he can help."

"I heard the lieutenant givin' him what-for this mornin'," Tony chuckled. "Seems the Air Police caught him in the club car havin' a drink last night."

"Oh," said Kirk. "So that's where he was. I know he hadn't come back when I went to bed. He finally told me his name—or rather his three names. It's Grant Boyd Castleman. He lives in some swanky suburb called Lake Forest."

Tony grinned. "Well," he said, "he's goin' to find things a little different in Basic. Wonder what he'll do when he finds the butler doesn't come when he rings!"

The berths weren't made up that night. "We'll be in San Antonio before long," the lieutenant told them after supper. "So there's no point in going to bed. You'll sleep on the base tonight."

He heaved a little sigh as he said it. Kirk could see that he would be heartily glad to be rid of his responsibility.

Ten o'clock came, and eleven, and still the train lumbered on through the Texas night. The recruits curled up on the seats as best they could and snored or talked in low voices. Then somebody—Kirk thought it was the quiet colored boy —began to play softly on a harmonica. He played it well. Soon they were singing along with him. The sleepers roused up, but nobody complained about the music.

Finally the concert died out and the snores resumed. Kirk was asleep when the train slowed down and jolted over switch points. A loud voice woke him.

"Come on, everybody! Get yourselves together. It's oh-one hundred, and we're in San Antone!"

He got his bag from under the seat and stood up in the aisle with the others.

"This is it," called an Air Police noncom from the vestibule. "You'll march out an' line up on the platform. Try to look like airmen!"

The train halted, the car door was opened, and they all began to shuffle down the aisle, yawning, blinking, their clothes rumpled and their hair falling in their eyes.

Kirk wasn't fully awake till he stood outside with the rest. It was a clear, starlit night, surprisingly cool. There were several officers and noncoms in Air Force uniforms there on the platform.

"Form up in line," bawled a sergeant. He was counting out loud as they took their places. "Sixty-six!" he called at last. "There's your flight, sir. Here comes the next batch."

A young-looking first lieutenant stepped in front of the line.

"All right, boys," he said in a clear voice. "You're members of a flight, and you'll stay together from now on. We won't bother with a roll call now, but I'd like to welcome you to Lackland—the finest training base in America. You're here to become airmen. When you make it, you can be proud of the name. It stands for one of the real key jobs in the defense of this country we love. I won't kid you. The training isn't easy. Sometimes you'll wish you were home working eight hours a day for more money. But if you've got the right stuff in you, you'll be real men when you come out. Now come on over this way. The first two buses are yours."

Kirk had been with Tony and Elmer when they lined up. He was still with them as they hurried toward the big, waiting buses. The driver of the first one was an Airman, First

Class. He counted to thirty-three and shut the door. Kirk made it, along with his two friends. The lieutenant and sergeant in charge of their flight were getting into a jeep to lead the way.

They rolled out of the city and down a broad, straight highway. Kirk, one of the last in, was seated near the front. He leaned forward and asked the driver a question.

"How far is it to the base?" he said.

"Seven miles," was the laconic reply. Then the man chuckled. "What's the matter, kid? Wasn't there a boy's room on the train?"

Those within hearing distance guffawed, and Kirk decided from then on to keep his mouth shut. By the time they stopped at the main gate his embarrassment was gone. There was a sign above the entrance. "Gateway to the Air Force," it read.

"Gosh!" he told himself with a little shiver. "This is it! I guess I'm on my way."

Kirk had an impression of an immense area full of streets and buildings. The bus pulled up in front of one of the larger structures.

"This is the reception center," the driver announced. "Pile out an' wait in line. The sarge'll tell you what to do."

The jeep had stopped just ahead of them. When both buses had discharged their passengers, the sergeant walked to the middle of the long line. His first words were a surprise.

"Anybody hungry?" he barked, and a mumbled chorus answered, "You bet!"—"Yes, sir!"—"I'll say we are!"

"Okay," said the sergeant. "Follow me. For'ard—hup!"

Their introduction to Lackland, in the wee hours of the morning, was steak—real steak—mashed potatoes, peas, rolls, milk, and heaped-up servings of ice cream. Somebody in the Air Force, Kirk thought as he finished off the meal, understood the needs of a bunch of healthy youngsters.

Afterward they were marched down the street to the long two-story frame building that would be their home for the next few months. There were rows of double-decker beds with neatly folded bedding piled on them. Tony and Kirk tossed a quarter, and Kirk won. He took the lower bed, and the young Italian climbed into the one above him. Elmer was close by, across the narrow dividing space. Inside of ten minutes everybody was asleep.

What seemed only a moment later Kirk half woke to a sound of distant bugles. The big room was still shadowy with the first gray of dawn. He rolled over and was instantly asleep again.

The recruits were given a break that morning. It wasn't until six o'clock—0600 in Air Force lingo—that the sergeant got them out of bed. "I let you skip reveille," he said. "From now on you'll be out two hours earlier. Come on— get shaved an' dressed. You're due at breakfast in twenty minutes."

There were eight washbasins for the sixty-six of them. That meant standing in line and shaving over each other's shoulders. It was a real scramble that first morning, but somehow they made it. In the bright, hot daylight they trotted over to the mess hall and got their breakfast. Then, under the watchful eye of the sergeant and an Airman, First Class, they policed their barracks. Most of them were sloppy bedmakers, but the noncoms soon changed that. Kirk got his bed approved on the second try. It took Grant Castleman longer, and he was white with pent-up fury when the Flight was finally called out to stand formation.

They had their first official roll call.

"Now," said the sergeant, when the last name was called and answered, "you're going to be processed. Before you get through, you won't know which end is up, but don't worry. A lot of guys have been processed before an' survived. Just keep moving an' go where you're told."

From just behind him, Kirk heard a rumble. It was the big colored boy, whose name, he had learned, was Corny Jones.

"Don't like that word!" Jones murmured. "Processin' is what my Pappy does in the stockyards—to hogs!"

4

It started painlessly enough. The Flight was ushered into a room full of chairs and told to sit down. Their lieutenant—the same one who had welcomed them at the train—came in briskly, smiled at their anxious faces, and gave them a brief run-down on what processing was all about.

"The Air Force has to do things systematically," he explained. "You'll understand later why all this is necessary. For the moment, whether you see the reasons or not, all you have to do is follow orders and keep the line moving. All right, Sergeant, take over."

Under the lieutenant's eye they lined up smartly. The first step was to get their military records started—the records that would follow them throughout their Air Force service. At a battery of typewriters, each operated by an Airman, Second, the boys answered a rapid fire of questions, and the answers were typed on the proper forms.

Then they moved into the next room. Nobody had mentioned the fact that one of the first steps in processing was to get paid. It came as something of a shock, but a pleasant one. They were fingerprinted and signed their names. Their first $10.00 was put in their hands.

With the happy glow still on them, they marched into still another room. A serious-faced young chaplain told them something about Air Force life. "You're of different faiths," he said. "That doesn't concern me. The main thing is that you believe and that you hold fast to your beliefs through these trying months when you're being turned into real airmen. You'll find things that bother you. If you think you're in trouble—if anything perplexes you—my door is always open. I can't promise I'll know all the answers, but I'll do my best to help."

He shook hands with each of them in turn and gave each a small Bible or other holy book appropriate to the boy's religious training. They were quiet and thoughtful as they left, impressed by the man's sincerity.

There was a break for noon chow at this point, but as soon as they had eaten, they were back in the processing line. They shuffled into another room and stared at the row of white pedestal chairs.

"For gosh sakes!" Tony Canuso gasped. "It's a barbershop!"

Those were the quickest haircuts Kirk ever saw. A few of the recruits had crew cuts when they reached the base. Most of them, including himself, wore their hair longer, and a few had ducktails and fancy sideburns. It was these who groaned loudest as they realized what was happening.

The barbers—there were two of them—didn't fool around with shears. They used the clippers, up the back and over the top, while the long, wavy locks fell in a cascade on the apron. It took about thirty seconds for each youth, and they all looked alike when they got out of the chairs. Not a hair remaining on their heads was more than half an inch long.

Two or three rebelled at this treatment. One who created a disturbance was Grant Boyd Castleman, who seemed to

feel his curly, carefully tended blond head was in some way
sacred. A sharp, quick word from the sergeant straightened
him out. A moment later he, too, was shorn. For all the good
it did him, his name might have been Joe Doaks.

There was some horseplay, and a few uncomplimentary
remarks were made before the operation was finished.
Standing in the line, Tony rubbed a hand playfully over the
bristles on Kirk's head.

"Boy, oh boy!" he snickered, "if you don't look like a
two-minute egg!"

"Okay, billiard ball," the boy answered with a grin.
"Wait till you get a good look at yourself in the mirror.
You're no movie star either."

Only young Castleman took no part in the general kidding. His face, below its denuded scalp, was scowling and
sullen.

"It's an outrage!" Kirk heard him mutter. "Our family
lawyer'll hear about this. Ought to sue 'em."

The sergeant had been standing close, and he, too, must
have overheard.

"Look, sonny," he said quietly. "You'll be grateful for a
short haircut when your regular schedule starts. There'll be
mighty little time in it for primpin', I can tell you. Besides,
you haven't lost it forever. Hair keeps growin', you know."

The last clipped recruits straggled sheepishly into the
line.

"All right." The sergeant raised his voice. "Next stop,
strip an' shower. Right through here. For'ard—hup!"

He steered them into a room with a row of shower heads
along one wall. "Hang your clothes right here," he told
them, indicating a line of hooks. "They'll be all right. I'll
keep an eye on 'em. Get yourselves good an' clean now.
You're goin' to try on some new clothes."

They bathed and toweled themselves dry. The noncoms

handed them duffel bags and told them to put their civilian clothes into them. Then they were marched, naked as newborn babes, into another room where tables were piled with clothing. From the skin out they were issued garments to fit—underwear, socks, khaki fatigues, caps, brogans. The dress uniforms would come later. These were their working clothes. They were measured quickly and accurately, and every figure was put down on paper. Kirk thought his heavy GI shoes felt a little big, but the airman who had measured his feet assured him they would fit after a week or two of drill.

They put on the new outfits, lined up again, and were marched back to their barracks, duffel bags over their shoulders.

"Now—" the sergeant told them cheerfully, when they were once more in the big dormitory room—"now you're going to get squared away. There by each bed you'll see a foot locker. There's a place in it for everything you own. Come here and I'll show you."

He picked one of the boys at random, took everything out of his bag, and went ahead with the demonstration. Civvies and other personal belongings were folded neatly and stored on the bottom. Then came the newly issued clothing, all packed in a special order. The top compartment was for writing materials, toilet articles, and other necessities. Kirk watched carefully. When the sergeant had finished, he and the others attempted to do the same thing with their own lockers. After two or three tries they had them packed to their instructor's satisfaction.

"I wouldn't guarantee they'd pass a real inspection," he remarked. "But they're not bad for the first time. Now, men, you've had a busy day. You've got an hour's free time before supper. The day room's right through here, an' it's a good place to take it easy when you've got the chance."

Some of them preferred to fling themselves on their beds, but most of the boys crowded into the day room. It was well fitted out with upholstered settees and chairs, a table for magazines and several small writing desks. At one end there was even a small soda fountain which became instantly popular.

Kirk plumped himself down on one of the settees, and the sergeant sat down beside him.

"Your name's Owen, isn't it?" the noncom asked. "I got word you were coming from a friend o' mine named Nelson, up at Jennison AFB. That's near your home town, I guess. My name's Breck. Nelson and I came in together, back in 'forty."

Kirk tried not to show his surprise. "Gee," he said. "I'm glad to meet you, sir. I've got a couple of questions. All this is sort of new to me."

"Never mind the 'sir,' " Breck chuckled. "That's for officers. Go ahead an' shoot."

"Well," Kirk hesitated, "I wanted to write home an' tell 'em my address. Maybe it's on my service papers, but I can't figure out just what it is."

"They just write your name and your Air Force serial number after it. Then Flight C, 3419th Student Squadron, Lackland AFB, Texas. Want to jot that down?"

Kirk did so gratefully. "Another thing," he said. "I thought we'd get a physical check-up an' shots an' so on before we did anything else."

"Just wait till tomorrow," the sergeant told him with a grin. "Shots? Boy, you'll wish you'd never heard the word!"

He strolled off to talk to other recruits, and Kirk penned a hasty note to his mother, giving her the address and announcing his safe arrival. He thought he had better wait till things settled down before he gave them the whole story.

After chow that night there was a briefing session about

the events of the next day, and they all turned in at 2100, which means nine o'clock.

There was no question about hearing the reveille bugle next morning. They were routed out at four, hustled into their fatigues, and stood early formation and roll call. Then, under the watchful eyes of the noncoms, they cleaned their barracks thoroughly, made their beds, and straightened out their belongings. When everything was neat as a pin, they were marched to the mess hall. Then back again for fifteen minutes in the barracks. By 0700 they were on their way to the physical examinations.

Heart, teeth, eyes, feet, weight, posture—there was an Air Force doctor to check on every one of these and more. Pages of medical history were added to their records. It was that day that they lost one of their original Flight members. He was the thin, quiet colored boy who played the harmonica. Kirk had heard him trying to smother his hollow coughing in the pillow the night before. He went home that afternoon with a medical discharge.

Kirk found out a lot of things about himself that day. His vision was 20-20 normal. His weight was five pounds under what it should be for his five-foot, ten-inch frame. His heart and lungs were O.K., and his blood type was A, with a positive RH factor. His teeth were all right for the present, but he would need a filling or two later. His reactions were quick; his blood pressure was just what it should be. Finally his feet were in good shape.

The last of the examining doctors glanced over Kirk's check list. "Good physical specimen," he nodded. "You'll put on the weight you need after a few weeks of drill and Air Force chow."

They had their first shots that afternoon. Some of the boys winced and turned pale when the needle went in. One or two had allergies that gave them a bad reaction and were sent to the base hospital for observation and further checking.

In the next two days they were given more processing, more shots, and a bewildering lot of information about the Air Force. There were lectures and training movies. There were formations several times a day, and when they marched to chow or classes, the sergeant began to insist that they keep the lines even and march in step.

"Everybody on the base can take one look and know you're recruits," he said. "I'm waitin' for the day when you begin to look like airmen."

Sunday came at last, and while it made little difference in the routine, Kirk did have time to write a long letter home. "It's pretty swell, here, really," he wound up his account. "The grub's good—not as good as your cooking, Mom, but there's plenty of it. We're all dog-tired by taps, so nobody has any trouble sleeping. And the fellows are a fine bunch, almost all of them. Even our sergeant is a good egg."

He was also given time to go to church that morning. With the other Protestants in his Flight he marched to a neat white-painted chapel where they sang hymns lustily and heard a good sermon. He felt well repaid when he came back to the barracks.

When reveille sounded at 0400 Monday morning, the sergeant had a word with them.

"Dress and clean up fast," he said. "Lieutenant Callan's coming in here right after formation. I want everything straightened up and looking smart."

They did their best. The lieutenant—the same one who had greeted them at the train—entered promptly at 0500, and they snapped to attention, each man standing rigid beside his bunk.

"I won't hold you up long," he told them. "We've just

had orders to accelerate training from thirteen weeks to eight. That means you'll work harder and learn faster than any training groups who've been here before. I think you can do it."

He paused, letting the words sink in. "I guess the reason for the speed-up is no secret," he went on. "War hasn't been declared. The fighting in Korea is officially a police action by the United Nations. But off the record I can tell you our forces are getting the living tar beaten out of them. That won't keep on. We're sending more infantry, more guns, and more airplanes over there. That's why you may be needed in a hurry. All right, Sergeant. Get some breakfast into these men."

It was a sober bunch of youngsters who marched to the mess hall. And before that long day ended, they knew there was no fooling about the accelerated program. It started with two hours of military drill—forming squads, marching, wheeling, standing attention, chests out and stomachs in. Then came physical training, with half an hour of calisthenics and a run. While they stood puffing after this exercise, the sergeant gave them some instruction in military discipline and courtesy.

After that they went over to get their dog tags and more shots. And right after noon chow there was a lecture on personal hygiene. Kirk hoped the ideas would sink in, for a couple of boys in the Flight seemed to know very little about bathing and keeping clean. One of them had even asked him what his toothbrush was for.

Another session of military drill followed, and they returned to the barracks—not to rest but to give the place a real old-fashioned cleaning. They scrubbed the floors inch by inch, and the windows were washed, outside and in.

Even the big, rugged fellows like Elmer Gamble and Corny Jones were bushed that night. They crawled into bed, too tired to roughhouse, too tired even to grumble, and slept like logs till dawn.

The day had been a fair sample of what was in store for them in the next eight weeks. It wasn't all drill or physical labor, though they had plenty of that. They had to use their minds and memories, too. Several hours of classroom work were held daily under businesslike instructors. Kirk had the advantage of his college training and kept alert. He knew he had to get everything possible out of the shortened course if he wanted to do well in Aircraft and Engine School, where he had his heart set on going.

He took full notes on everything that was told him, from facts about military intelligence and geopolitics to the care and handling of the .45 automatic and the M-2 carbine.

The physical training routine grew tougher as the days went by. One afternoon they marched a full ten miles, singing as they swung along in step. Corny Jones helped out there. He had a big, rich baritone voice and seemed to know instinctively what familiar tunes would fit the marching rhythm.

They ran the obstacle course, crawling through barrels on their bellies, scaling seven-foot walls, and crossing gullies hand over hand by means of ropes stretched overhead. There were other kinds of exercise as well. They played volleyball and baseball or put on the gloves and sparred. The boxing instructor was a fast-moving, wiry sergeant who had once been welterweight champion of the old Army Air Corps.

The first day he boxed, Kirk caught the sergeant's eye. "You ever done any o' this before?" the older man asked.

"A little," Kirk admitted. "I tried out for lightweight in college, but I didn't make the boxing team."

"You've got reach," said the sergeant, "an' quick hands.

Keep that left jab moving. Use your feet—like this—and get some steam into your punches. That's better."

He called a stocky young Italian over. The boy was shorter than Kirk but a few pounds heavier.

"Let's see you mix it for a round," the sergeant told them.

The other lad had little science but plenty of strength. He swung his gloved fists like clubs while Kirk danced away, keeping the long left in his face. When his baffled opponent stopped charging, Kirk stepped in fast. He jabbed once more to the face, crossed a right to the mid-section, and, when the other's guard dropped, swung a hard left hook to the side of his jaw.

It was a lucky blow. The headgear protected the Italian from any real damage, but there was force enough in the hook to knock him off balance. He sat down hard on the canvas, then scrambled up angrily.

"Hold it," snapped the sergeant. "That's enough for now."

He turned to Kirk. "What's your name?" he asked.

"Kirk Owen."

"K.O., huh? All right, Kayo, just so you don't get cocky, let's see you do that to me."

The lesson Kirk learned in the next two minutes was painful but probably good for him. He hardly laid a glove on the sergeant. Meanwhile, he was peppered with lefts and rights, to the obvious enjoyment of the young Italian.

At evening chow Kirk found he had a new nickname. From that time on he was known as Kayo to the members of C Flight.

5

On Saturday of his second week at Lackland, Kirk went over to the Base Exchange and weighed himself on the penny scales. He had put on four of the five needed pounds and had never felt better in his life. This, he decided, called for a banana split to celebrate.

On the stool next to his at the fountain was a girl about his own age. She was dressed in a neat WAF trainee's uniform, her cap perched jauntily on her blond curls. He had been aware of the presence of women on the base, but they kept to their own section. This was his first close-up of one of them.

"Hi," he said with a grin. "Aren't you off limits?"

She turned cornflower-blue eyes to his face. "Yes," she replied. "I needed something our store didn't have and got permission from the captain. Maybe I shouldn't have stopped for a soda, but it was mighty hot walking over. I suppose you're a trainee, too. My name's Ginnie Gordon. What's yours?"

He told her. By the time his split was ready, they knew quite a lot about each other. Ginnie was from Kansas. Her family had a small wheat farm, and she was the youngest of five sisters. The others had gone to college, but when she graduated from high school, the money had run out. After a year of driving the tractor, she had decided to enlist.

She finished her soda and stood up. "Hope I'll see you again, Kirk," she smiled. "The Service Club dances aren't bad. Or if you should happen to get a pass the same time I do, we could see what San Antone's historic landmarks look like."

"Sounds wonderful," he said. "I'll make it if I can. How do I get in touch with you?"

They exchanged mailing addresses, and she departed, looking slim and cool and pretty. Kirk whistled to himself under his breath. He was glad the rest of the gang hadn't been there to spoil his encounter.

Two weeks went by before he had a chance to see the girl again, and in the meantime a lot of things happened. One of them was a series of classification tests. From some of the questions asked him, Kirk had a momentary idea that the officers might be thinking of him as cadet material. Then he remembered the rule that required two full years of college credits and resolutely put it out of his mind. He was happy when it appeared he qualified for Aircraft and Engine training. That was what he wanted, he told himself— A & E School.

The tough grind proceeded without a letup. One or two of the youngsters in Flight C rebelled, cut formations, and had to walk a lot of miles on guard duty. A handful of others were discharged—two for lying about their age and one because he had failed to report a term in jail for car-stealing. But for the most part, the Flight was proving itself able to take the accelerated training.

KP was a duty everybody shared in turn. The two days Kirk spent in the mess kitchen were eye openers to him. The big stainless steel kettles and ovens were kept as clean as hospital equipment, and the vegetables that came in daily were of top quality. He knew because he helped peel and prepare bushels of them. In the huge freezer he found prime beef, pork, and lamb, and anybody could see that the Air Force spared no expense in the grade of food it provided.

The only trouble was the cooking. Preparing meals in the big quantities necessary seemed to take out some of the flavor. Also, although the head cook was a well-trained expert, his assistants were green and sometimes clumsy. On the whole, Kirk thought it was amazing the chow tasted as good as it did.

During the fourth week C Flight was marched down to the target range and given firing instructions with the carbine. Shooting for record on the range would come later. Kirk looked forward to that. He knew he had a good eye, for he had used a .22 rifle since he was twelve. The M-2 was a comfortable little gun in his hands, and he got the trick of the slow trigger squeeze without difficulty.

He was far too busy during the day and too tired at night to do much mooning about the WAF from Kansas. But the memory of her blue eyes and friendly smile stayed with him. He managed to get off for one of the dances at the Service Club. There were plenty of attractive girls there— town girls and officers' daughters for the most part—but no WAF trainees attended on that particular night. He had a few dances and came back to barracks.

Then, at mail call one Saturday morning, he got a note in a small, square envelope, addressed in a feminine hand. "I've got a one-day pass for Sunday," it said. "If you could possibly wangle one, we could spend the day in town. I'll be at the bus stop at Gate Two at eight-thirty." It was signed "Virginia Gordon."

As soon as he had a moment free, Kirk hurried to the day room and saluted the lieutenant smartly. "Recruit Owen, Flight C, sir," he introduced himself. "Requesting a pass for San Antonio tomorrow, sir."

It was the first time he had asked for any privileges, and his knees shook a little. The lieutenant looked him up and down, then leafed through a stack of records on the table.

"Hm," he said, "Owen, Kirk. No marks against you. Any particular reason for the pass?"

"Y-yes, sir. A friend of mine is going to be in town."

The officer repressed a smile. Kirk knew he had a pretty fair idea about the "friend."

"Permission granted," said the lieutenant with a nod. "I'll make it for twelve hours, starting at oh-eight hundred. Here you are, and don't get in trouble."

At ten minutes past eight the next morning Kirk showed his pass to the gate guard and stepped off the base. The air didn't feel any different outside, but he drew a deep breath of it nevertheless. He was free and on his own for the first time in a month. His uniform was neatly pressed, his shoes were well shined, and he was wearing the blue

Air Force cap. The sun was bright, but it was cool for San Antonio.

Down at Gate Two he saw a bevy of a dozen WAF trainees, all dressed in their best. There were fat ones and thin ones, plain ones and attractive ones, but no Ginnie. Disconsolate, he stood a few yards away from the group looking now and then at the wrist watch he had put on for the occasion.

At eight-thirty he could see the bus rolling up the highway. Just as he was trying to decide whether to board it, there was a flurry at the gate, and a lone WAF came flying across the road. It was Ginnie. She panted a greeting, and they climbed aboard in the wake of the other girls. They were lucky to get a seat together before the bus filled up with male recruits at the next gate.

Flushed from her dash, he thought she was prettier than ever. The delay, she hastened to explain, was due to remembering her camera at the last minute and having to dig it out of her locker. She showed it to him, a plain little box camera that fitted into her shoulder bag.

"What do you want to do, Kirk?" she asked. "Maybe I can steer you. I've seen the sights before."

"I'll leave everything to you, then," he told her. "Just being off the base and having you to talk to is enough to make it a big day."

They wandered past the big stores, window-shopping and conversing. They went out to a park where they rode on some of the amusement concessions, ate hot dogs and cones, and drank cokes. And as a climax they visited the Alamo. Though it was right in the midst of the city, there was a solemn hush in the ancient structure. Light filtered down through the overhead beams of the arcade. They took each other's pictures standing in front of the old Spanish masonry and persuaded an attendant to take a snapshot of them together. Finally they went to a movie.

The newsreel showed films of the fighting in Korea. Kirk squirmed in his seat, and the girl touched his arm companionably. "I know," she whispered. "You feel as if you ought to be there. Well, I hope it's over before you have to go."

"Maybe," he answered. "But it's not going to be quick or easy. I'd sure like to be working on those jet fighters—keeping 'em in shape."

It was nearly six when they came out of the theater. They ate chow mein in a little Chinese restaurant and rode back to Lackland together on the bus.

"Gosh, Ginnie," said Kirk, as they neared his gate. "I haven't had a nicer day since I can remember. Will you write to me?"

"Yes," she told him simply. "It's been grand." And just before he got off, she gave his hand an impulsive little squeeze.

That was the last glimpse he had of her for a long time. She wrote, though—good long letters that he answered in kind. A week later she had sent him prints of the snapshots. The one he had taken of her he put carefully in his wallet. She looked cool and clear-eyed and beautiful—just the way he wanted to remember her. The picture of them together wasn't quite as good, but he mailed it home with a full account of their twelve-hour pass. "I hope you like her, Mom," he wrote. "She's the kind of girl I want to marry some day."

*   *   *

During the sixth week of training, Flights A, B, and C went out for an overnight bivouac. They carried full packs and helmets and marched twelve miles to a wild section of mesquite and brush. It wasn't accomplished without some grousing. The heat made them sweat, and several of the boys announced they hadn't joined the Air Force to be dough-faced mud soldiers. Weren't they ever going to see any airplanes?

When they got to their destination, they found water— a small spring in an otherwise dry canyon—set up their pup tents, dug latrines, and ate the sketchy chow provided by the field kitchens. The Texas night was full of stars. Off on a rise of ground half a mile away a coyote howled dolefully. With the darkness a chill had fallen over the desert.

They were given a refresher talk on survival and turned in. Kirk had camped out before and was enjoying himself, but some of the city-bred youngsters were less at ease. From the next tent he could hear Corny Jones's plaintive voice. "Don't reckon I'm goin' to sleep at all," the big colored lad was saying. "That doggone wolf, he gives me the creeps!"

At dawn they were roused out and discovered what it was like to wash in a helmet half-full of water. After formation and breakfast they were given some military skirmish workouts and hiked back to the base feeling like hardened airmen.

It was early in the seventh week that Tony Canuso got together a baseball team to play B Flight. Because they had only a little over an hour to play, it was limited to six innings. In the top of the sixth, with the visitors leading by a run, Flight C's pitcher got a sore arm, and Tony looked about in desperation for a replacement. He was about to move in from shortstop and take the mound himself when Grant Castleman approached him.

"I used to pitch a little in prep school," the Lake Forest boy said. "I'll try it if you'd like."

Tony hesitated. "Okay," he replied. "Let's see what you've got."

It turned out he had quite a lot, including a good fast ball, a sinker, and fair control. There was one out with two on when he started. He walked the first man to load the bases, then proceeded to strike out the next two batters.

Tony got aboard with an infield single in the final half-inning, and Corny Jones belted a tremendous line drive over the center fielder's head to win the ball game.

"You know," Tony told Kirk afterward, "that Castleman kid surprised me. He's no panty-waist. Maybe the Air Force'll make a real guy out of him yet."

The final week of training came, and the results of the classification test went up on the board. Out of a possible 9-point score, Kirk found he had been given an 8.7—one of the best ratings in his Flight. He had requested A & E training, and it was no surprise when he was told he had been posted to Sheppard Air Force Base in North Texas.

It was a proud group of young men who stood in trim ranks for their last Retreat. Kirk stole a glance along the line and thought back to the shambling crowd that had come off the train only two months before. The change was hard to believe.

Bugles began to play the soft, solemn notes, and the flag came slowly down, its stars and stripes still shining in the afterglow.

6

Kirk's travel orders allowed him forty-eight hours to report to his new base. It wasn't long enough for even a flying visit to his home, and the trip north to Wichita Falls would take only eight or ten hours by train. So he packed and hung around the barracks, more or less at a loose end.

There were six others from C Flight with orders to move on to Sheppard. They were killing time in the day room that afternoon when Sergeant Breck came in. He grinned at the lolling boys.

"Takin' it easy, huh?" he asked. "Well, you've earned it, the way we had to drive you. All of you here are headed for A & E School at Sheppard, an' I thought maybe you'd like to go in style. There's a war-weary old C-47 takin' off for there at 0700. Friend o' mine's the pilot, an' he says he'll have room for a few more bodies. It won't be comfortable, but it's the Air Force way to travel. What do you say?"

All of them accepted. Right after breakfast next morning they rode over to the field in a truck and were hustled up the ramp into the transport plane, duffel bags and all.

Kirk's heart was beating fast. He had never had a chance to fly before. More by luck than good management he got a seat on the side bench next to a window, just forward of

the wing. Fastening his seat belt, he leaned close to the
glass, watching the ground crew as they took away the gas
truck and the first engine was started. As the propeller
began to turn lazily and the engine took hold with a grunt
and a roar, he became aware of someone beside him. Looking around, he saw it was Grant Boyd Castleman.

The blond youngster grinned. "Hi, Kayo," he said. "We
seem to get together when we travel, don't we? This ought
to be better than that train trip anyhow."

"Yeah—and quicker. I reckon you've gone a lot o' places
by air before, haven't you?"

"Well, yes," Castleman replied. "Quite a few. Mother
and I flew to Europe last summer. And the Christmas before
that we went to Hawaii. Down to Mexico City, too, when I
was a kid. I've always liked it. Maybe that's why I picked
the Air Force."

He wasn't boasting, Kirk realized. There had been a
surprising change in the boy since those first days at Lack-

land, and it went deeper than the short-clipped hair and worn fatigues. Grant had turned into a pretty good recruit.

The chocks were removed, and the old transport lumbered into motion. They taxied down-field, swung around to warm up the engines, and started their take-off run with a businesslike roar. Kirk felt a tingle down his spine as they picked up speed. The tail came up, and the runway whizzed past in a blur. He held his breath, waiting. Then, before he knew it, they were air-borne, climbing steadily into the blue.

"Gosh!" he said, shakily. "We're flying—easy as that!"

Grant's laugh was understanding. "Sure," he answered. "A good pilot makes the take-off feel simple enough. Wish I could be one myself."

"So do I," said Kirk from the bottom of his heart.

The flight took only about three hours, and they had ample time to find their barracks, stow their duffel, and report in at Squadron Headquarters on the new base. Elmer Gamble was among the little group of newcomers—the only one of Kirk's close friends who had been sent to Sheppard. Together they toured the base after noon chow. Then, not to waste their last bit of free time, they took a bus into Wichita Falls for supper.

"Well," said the big farmer boy when they got back to barracks, "this won't be quite as nice as we had it at Lackland. But I reckon we'll be too busy to notice. From what I've seen, it looks like a real workin' base, an' that suits me. The sooner I learn enough to be some real use, the better I'll like it."

Sheppard was indeed a working base, as they found out after reveille next morning. Breakfast was at 0500. As soon as the barracks were policed, they got a briefing by their new flight lieutenant.

"You men look healthy," he said. "That's good, because the next twenty-six weeks are going to be tough. You won't get as much physical training as you've been used to nor as many drills and parades. But there'll be more classroom study, more demonstrations, and then some real practical work in the shops. This course is in fourteen phases. In one you'll learn about aircraft structures; another, electronics; a third, hydraulics—and so on. Finally you'll have two phases on jet engines and two on piston engines. When you get through, if you've done your job, you'll be able to pull an engine change on an F-84 jet or a B-29 bomber. And if you pass your final test, you'll graduate out of Tech TAF. All right, let's go."

The first lecture that morning was four hours long and dealt with principles of aerodynamics. By the time Kirk got out, his brain was spinning with the facts and theories he had tried to absorb.

Elmer Gamble grinned at him and shook his head. "Think you know what makes an airplane fly?" he asked. "Hanged if I do, but they tell me the doggone things get up in the air somehow."

That afternoon there was more of the same, after which they were marched over to a big hangar and shown the actual shapes of aircraft at close range. The demonstration helped Kirk. He began to sort out some of the scientific words he had heard and make sense out of them.

He turned in early that night, but before he did, he wrote two letters. One was to his mother, telling about his arrival at Sheppard and what life was like there. The other was to Ginnie Gordon. He had tried to call her before he left Lackland but was unable to reach her. At least he wanted her to know where he was.

*   *   *

Before he had been at Sheppard a week, Kirk felt at home in his new surroundings. He had a better trained mind than some of his classmates, and instead of being bored by the lectures and technical movies, he found himself enjoying them. Best of all, though, was the practice work they did. First on mockups, then on actual airplanes, the trainees were given simple assignments under the watchful eyes of veteran airmen.

They studied the control systems that operated flaps and stabilizers and landing gear. They traced fuel lines from wing tanks to engines. And for many days they sweated over the intricate wiring of electrical systems, taking out and replacing the miles of colored wire that ran like nerves from the "brain" of the instrument panel to other parts of the airplane.

Engines were a whole field of study by themselves. When Kirk thought of the pride he had taken in souping up the motor of his little car, he had to laugh. It had been ridiculously easy compared to the simplest operation on one of those giant engines that turned the props of a B-29.

After the near-tropical climate of San Antonio, the boys found the North Texas autumn raw and harsh. There had been a few hot days in September, but the nights soon grew colder, and one late October morning there was frost on the ground when they marched to chow. A month later Kirk had his first experience of a Texas "norther." Stinging dust, driven by a vicious wind, blew down across the base for two days. Then came a cold, bone-chilling rain. They shivered in their raincoats and ran between classes to keep warm.

But weather made no difference in the activity of the base. Planes came skittering in on the wet runways or took off with a roar of engines night and day. They always seemed to be in a hurry. There was a feeling of urgency in the air, and it communicated itself to the youngsters who were learning to be mechanics.

They had a fair idea of what was going on in Korea. When the Allied Forces had recovered from the first jolt and started pushing north toward the Yalu, air support was needed more than ever. That was why increasing numbers of B-29 bombers were being recommissioned and more jet fighters readied for duty.

One of the greatest needs, the boys were told by their instructors, was more air transport. Thousands of tons of precious aircraft parts, engines, medical supplies, and blood plasma had to be rushed to the front, halfway around the world.

That was when Kirk saw his first C-97. The big, double-decked MATS cargo plane roared in one evening for a fast overhaul and took off again shortly after dawn. A crack ground crew had worked on her all night.

"Look at her!" the veteran crew chief bragged. "Two days an' she'll be in Japan. What a workhorse!"

Thanksgiving came and passed, hardly noticed in the rush of work except for the turkey and cranberry sauce they had for dinner. Once a week the Flight was given a short briefing session on events at the front. They had no time to read the newspapers, so that was all they knew about the Korean fighting. It was at the first such session in December that Kirk heard a new and ominous word. It was the name of a fighter plane—the MIG-15.

"Up to now," the serious-faced young lieutenant told them, "our fighters have been meeting pretty second-rate stuff—mostly YAKS and IL-10's. A month ago we'd shot down so many of them that you could almost say the North Korean Air Force was destroyed. Anyhow, they've been able to do very little damage. From now on it may be different. Since the Chinese Reds came in, the Russians seem to be giving them the MIG-15 jet in considerable numbers. And let me tell you, this is quite an airplane. Here's a picture of it drawn from the best information we have."

He had the drawing flashed on the screen. "It doesn't look like so much," he went on. "Nothing revolutionary about its lines. It's lighter and smaller than our newest jets. And it can climb faster, maneuver better. It packs a wallop in those 20-millimeter and 37-millimeter cannon. They got one of our B-29's early in November. The tail gunner in another B-29 shot down our first MIG a few days later, but it fell behind the lines, where we couldn't get at it.

"Our main disadvantage against the MIG's," he continued, "is geography. All their bases are in Manchuria, across the Yalu, and we're forbidden to follow them there. What's been happening so far is something like this. The MIG squadrons stay back there, ready, until their observers spot some of our planes coming in for bombing or strafing missions. Then they fly north out of sight and go up to altitudes well above us. The first thing our pilots know, here come the little devils, diving out of nowhere at 600 knots. That's so fast that seconds after they're sighted they're firing.

"Our F-80's can take them on—give them quite a fight, as a matter of fact. But the minute the Reds see that things are going against them, they scoot back over the Yalu and thumb their noses at us."

Kirk raised his hand. "What about these new F-86 jets?" he asked the instructor. "Won't they be able to handle the MIG's better than F-80's and F-84's?"

The lieutenant smiled. "You're a step ahead of me," he replied. "I can tell you this. There are F-86-A's in Korea now. Before Christmas we ought to have some combat reports."

Kirk hadn't been close to an F-86-A yet. But he had seen

one take off half a mile away and heard the vicious whine of its big jet engine. Soon, he hoped, they'd have an F-86 in the shop, where he and his classmates could work on it.

He had followed the progress of this strange war week by week in the briefing sessions. There had been some bad days back in August, when the outmanned Allied troops had been pushed back and back, almost into the sea at Pusan. Then came the grim holding action and the turn of the tide when the North Korean Reds had overextended their supply lines. Air power, he knew, had been the biggest factor in smashing those lines. By mid-September the UN forces were advancing steadily. After the surprise landing at Inchon, the advance moved faster, and before October ended, it looked as if the North Koreans would be shoved clear back to the Yalu boundary.

Then suddenly the whole complexion of the struggle changed. A horde of Chinese Red "volunteers" came swarming down from Manchuria—tough, well-trained troops with modern artillery and tanks. And the Allied forces found they had all they could do to hold their gains.

As Christmas drew near, Kirk had just a touch of homesickness. It had always been a happy time at home, and this year would be different. He knew that even if he was given a two-day pass he couldn't get to Clarksdale and back.

Mr. Owen had gone back to work on a part-time basis, but Kirk continued to send home half of his modest pay every month. Until now it hadn't bothered him to have so little money left over. He was too busy to spend much anyway. But when he tried to pick out Christmas gifts for his family, he wished he had a few more dollars.

At the Base Exchange he finally bought a pair of fleece-lined slippers for his father and a small electric iron for his mother. For Margie he'd been saving a book, "My Life at Lackland," filled with pictures of the training program at the big San Antonio base.

With just two dollars left, he started looking for something to send Ginnie Gordon. She had sent him a brief note late in November, telling him she had completed her training and was being shipped out to some post in the Pacific. Just where she didn't know, but she gave him an address, care of the Postmaster in San Francisco.

The selection of "Gifts for Ladies" seemed to be mostly perfume and lingerie, neither of which seemed quite appropriate. After long searching he found a little silver compact with Air Force wings embossed on its top. He wasn't sure whether she would like it, but it was the best he could do, and he put it hopefully in a well-wrapped box and sent it off.

Mail call the day before Christmas was a big event. It took the better part of an hour to pass out all the packages and letters that had come for the Flight.

Kirk opened his gifts with mixed feelings. He was pleased with the things his mother and father had sent him, and the Toll-House cookies that Margie had baked with her own hands were wonderfully good. But he felt a long way from home. The last small package he opened was from Ginnie. It was a slim little leather folder with space in it for two photographs. One of the pictures was the snapshot they had had taken together at the Alamo. The other was a posed portrait of the young WAF in uniform—a smiling, clear-eyed picture, as cool and fresh as appleblossoms on a May morning.

Most of the boys in the barracks had pin-up girl photographs in their lockers. Kirk would have been proud to show his own, but instead he tucked the little wallet neatly away in the pocket of his dress blouse. This was a pretty good Christmas after all, he thought.

7

By mid-January the Flight was well along in the second phase of the course on piston engines. They had disassembled, studied, and put back together an old engine from a wartime B-24. Now they were going through the same process with the bigger, more powerful B-29 engine.

One frosty morning, as Kirk trotted across to the shops, he caught a glimpse of a noncom entering the door ahead of him. There was something familiar about the man's easy, erect carriage and the jaunty angle of his cap. He was talking to the captain in charge of the program when Kirk got inside, but the boy had a good look at his square-jawed face. It was his old friend, Sergeant Ivar Nelson.

Five minutes later the sergeant was introduced to the group as their new instructor.

"Form up, men," he ordered with a smile. "Sound off with your names. I'll want to know who I'm talking to."

He walked down the line, looking into each boy's face and nodding as he heard the name. Kirk was poker-faced as he gave his. The sergeant hesitated only a fraction of a second, then moved on. But Kirk saw the wink that accompanied his nod.

Later, when the boy was polishing a piston, Nelson stopped a moment to watch him work. "I see you made it," he grinned. "I figured you'd be picked for A & E, but it's pure luck finding you here at Sheppard. Here, let me show you a trick with that."

As he worked over the piston, he filled Kirk in on the past five months.

"Air Police duty got me down," he explained. "I wanted

something steadier and more use to the service. So I put in for crew chief. They didn't have anything open right then, but they offered me this job. It's a chance to get my hand in again, so I took it. My wife'll be moving down here next month with the kids."

"I've been 'round to see your folks a couple of times," he went on, "and they're fine. Your father's really trying to take care of himself. He feels better all the time. When you write home, give 'em all my regards."

The sergeant seemed to take a special interest in Kirk's Air Force career. They talked a few minutes nearly every day, and when the boy was discouraged over his classwork or a tough mechanical problem in the shop, Nelson quickly snapped him out of it and made him feel ashamed of his mood.

In February the Nelson family arrived and moved into a small frame house in the noncommissioned officers' area near the base. One Saturday night Kirk was invited over there to supper. The moment he got inside the door he felt at home.

Olga Nelson was a tall, pleasant-faced young woman of Norse descent, like her husband. In spite of having two rollicking youngsters to handle, she was calmly efficient, and her house was as neat as a pin. When she spoke, the little boys minded instantly.

She was a good cook, too. After months of mess-hall meals, Kirk enjoyed every mouthful of his supper. The men helped with the dishes; the small fry were put to bed; and then the three of them sat down to talk in the comfortable living room.

"You seem to like the Air Force," said Mrs. Nelson. "All set to be a mechanic, Ivar tells me. Don't you sometimes wish you could be flying instead?"

Kirk flushed and hesitated. He didn't want to hurt the sergeant's feelings, but he decided to be honest.

"Every time I see a plane take off," he said, "I wish I was up there at the controls. But I guess it's no use. They won't take you for an Aviation Cadet without two full years of college. Anyhow I can learn how to keep 'em flying."

Ivar Nelson took a long time lighting his pipe before he spoke. "I don't blame you, son," he said, when the old black briar was drawing. "You love speed. I knew it when I first saw you racing that rod o' yours. And don't think—just because I'm a ground mechanic—that I haven't felt the same way myself. When I hear one o' those new experimental jets cut in the afterburner an' blast upstairs, I'd give my right arm to be in the seat."

He lay back, puffing slowly at the pipe. "What sort o' grades did you have, Kirk—back at college?" he asked abruptly.

The boy was taken by surprise. "I—I don't know," he answered. "At midyear I was doing all right—had B's or B-plusses in all my courses. Why?"

"Nothing—just thinking about something else. Let's see what's on the radio. If there's a good band, Olga likes to dance."

That evening at the Nelsons' stood out as one of the bright spots in Kirk's life at Sheppard. There weren't many of them. For the most part he worked, with his hands and his head, twelve or fourteen tough hours a day. When he fell into the sack, he slept like a log, without dreaming, until reveille.

He saw a good bit of Elmer Gamble, who was in his section, and the better he came to know the big farm lad, the more he liked him. Grant Castleman had been fairly keen about the training at first. But the steady grind began to irk him before he had been there long. It was no surprise to Kirk when he heard that the Chicago boy had applied for transfer to another branch of the Air Force. There must have been some political wirepulling by his family. Anyhow, he departed in February, and nobody seemed to know where he had gone.

The Flight was working on jet engines now. Kirk was glad he had studied physics in college, for there was a lot of it involved in jet-propelled aircraft. In principle a turbojet engine looked simple enough compared to the reciprocating type. It had fewer moving parts and less bulk. But the design and metallurgy of rotor blades that had to spin at terrific speeds and withstand thousand-degree heat brought a train of new problems. In the same way, by doubling the speed of planes, jet propulsion called for new wing and body shapes and greater structural strength.

It was a proud day for the section when they pulled an engine change on an F-84 in close-to-record time. That was in March. They had completed all their course except for the final examination—the specialty test known as No. 43131. Passing it would mean graduation from Tech TAF and promotion.

For two days they sweated over review work, getting ready for the test. Kirk read and reread his notes. He and Elmer asked each other all the questions they could think of, and their heads were still spinning when they turned in at midnight.

Actually the test itself was easier than Kirk had expected. He was fairly certain he had passed, though some of the others in the Flight were gloomy about their scores.

"One thing sure," said Elmer with a wry grin. "Nobody's goin' to be flunked out o' the Air Force an' sent home. They'll find a job for us someplace."

They had to wait till afternoon of the next day to find out how they had done. When the test results went up on the bulletin board, they crowded around it ten deep. The men with high scores whooped in triumph or commiserated with their less fortunate mates. Kirk, trying to get close enough to read the names, heard someone call from up front.

"Look a' that Kayo boy! Top man in the whole shebang!"

"Sure," another voice replied. "He's a ringer! Went to college, didn't he?"

Elmer, taller than most of them, craned his neck till he could see the board. Then he turned with a grin. "Yippee!" he yelled. "Attaboy, Kirk! Eight-point-nine! Some score!"

Kirk didn't believe it till he saw it with his own eyes. Nobody ever got a nine, he had heard, but he had come mighty close. Reddening under the gibes and congratulations, he hurried off to the day room to write his family.

They had a little graduation ceremony that night, at which the captain told them they had passed a milestone. "You're Airmen, now," he said. "You've worked hard for it, and I know you'll bear the title proudly. Your next step will be Crew TAF training. You'll have two days' travel time to get to your next bases. Assignments will be given you at morning formation tomorrow. Dismissed."

*   *   *

The C-54 let down over the mountains and started its descent to the dusty brown plain that stretched away toward another distant range beyond. Kirk straightened himself and tightened his safety belt for the landing. He was wearing his carefully pressed blue uniform, and on his sleeve was something new—the circled star and single stripe of an Airman, Third Class.

As they rolled down the runway, the afternoon sun glinted on long rows of jet fighters along the flight line. Kirk couldn't take his eyes off them. It still seemed too good to be true that he had been sent here to Nellis AFB, the big F-86 base at Las Vegas, Nevada. He was the only one left of the original Clarksdale contingent. Elmer Gamble, who had made a better score in piston engines than in jets, was on his way to McConnell AFB in Kansas. During the months at Sheppard, Kirk had heard once or twice from Tony Canuso. The Italian boy had applied for food-service training and was taking a course at a special Air Force school in Illinois. However, among the A & E graduates Kirk had made a lot of new friends, and half a dozen of them were in the group sent to Nellis.

There was little formality in the reception they were given when they came down the ramp from the plane. A businesslike sergeant checked off their names on a list and led the way to a truck that carried them, with their duffel bags, to their new quarters. The barracks buildings were modern and well equipped but weather-beaten by the constantly blowing dust. Kirk could see that the spic-and-span neatness he had learned at Lackland would be harder to keep up here in the Nevada desert.

As evening came, they could see dazzling lights and a glow in the sky a few miles away. Over there, they were told, was Las Vegas with its blazing neon signs.

"That's bad medicine for Airmen," a Tech Sergeant told them with a grin. "A guy can drop a month's pay awful fast if he starts playin' those tables an' machines. Maybe rich folks can afford it, but nobody really wins in Las Vegas except the one-arm bandits."

"What about movies an' eats?" one of the new arrivals asked. "The town isn't off limits, is it?"

"Oh, you'll get some free time over there," the sergeant replied. "The chow's probably better right here on the base, an' the movies about as good. But you might get a look at a Hollywood star now an' then. The safest fun in Vegas is watchin' suckers lose their money."

Kirk was less interested in the wide-open gambling town than in the job he would be doing. It started with a briefing early next morning. Each of the newcomers, he learned, would be assigned to work with an experienced maintenance group servicing the Sabrejets that were used for advanced flight and gunnery training.

An hour later he found himself checking the landing gear of an F-86 under the critical eye of a hatchet-faced Tech Sergeant. The noncom's name was Claggett. He looked and acted like a slave driver, but even while Kirk smarted under his sharp-tongued criticism, he had to admit the man knew his business.

At noon chow Kirk asked an A 2/C who sat next to him if he had ever worked under Sergeant Claggett. The other man chuckled.

"Old Iron-jaw? You got him for an instructor? Well, you're lucky. The guy'll take the hide off you for doin' things the wrong way, but you'll be a real mechanic before you're through. Did you see the hash-marks he carries? Fifteen years in the Air Force! There isn't an airplane— World War or since—that he doesn't know inside an' out."

The new men from Sheppard didn't work in the hangars all the time. Each afternoon they had an hour or two of lectures and movies, for they were still undergoing training. There was time for physical exercise, too. Kirk played enough baseball to keep him fit, and his weight was up to the prescribed standard.

He had been at Nellis for three weeks when one of his flight-mates suggested an evening in Las Vegas. It was right after payday, and Kirk had a few dollars in his pocket, so he agreed.

They took a bus into town, and from the time they hit

the outskirts of the city itself, their eyes were popping. The whole place seemed to be strung out along Route 91. Gigantic signs, fifty feet and more in height, glared with more neon lights than Kirk had ever imagined. The boys got off the bus and walked slowly up the roaring "strip." It was like a traveling carnival multiplied a hundred times. Every store, restaurant, saloon, and swank hotel blared forth its inducements, trying to outdo the others.

They went into a big drugstore and ordered double chocolate shakes at the fountain. The place was lined with slot machines along both walls. Twenty or thirty people were playing the machines, and when Kirk's companion had gulped down his drink, he hurried to get five dollars worth of quarters.

The Clarksdale boy watched him while he dropped all twenty coins, one after another, in the slot without result. Kirk had a couple of quarters in change, and he decided that was all he was willing to gamble. He put the first one in and pulled the lever. Bells rang, lights blazed, and into the metal holder under the spout fell a cascade of bright silver.

"Why—" gasped his friend, "you lucky bum! Hit the jackpot! Count 'em an' see what you got."

There were forty-two quarters in the pot—ten dollars and a half. Kirk calmly carried them over to the cashier and had the ten dollars changed into bills.

"Come on," urged the other airman. "Your luck's in. Keep on hittin' 'em." But Kirk shook his head.

"Money means too much to me," he said. "I'm trying to help out a little at home. The ten bucks goes to my folks next time I write."

8

The dozen mechanics who worked with Kirk under Sergeant Claggett were put in charge of all maintenance on a pair of F-86 Sabrejets about the end of April. The youthful second lieutenants who flew them were freshly graduated from the Aviation Cadets and wore their bright new wings with a bit of justifiable swagger. They were at Nellis for final gunnery training before being sent across the Pacific.

Kirk was on speaking terms with both officers, but he liked one in particular. Lieutenant Peabody was an apple-cheeked young man from Maine. He spoke with a clipped New England twang that was hard for a Midwesterner like Kirk to get used to.

Peabody had left Bowdoin College in his junior year to enter the Cadets. He talked, ate, and slept flying, and he loved his airplane like a mother. That's how the two young men got acquainted. Peabody was always in the hangar when he had an hour off watching the mechanics work on his F-86 with a jealous eye. Kirk, by the same token, would follow the jet out to the flight line whenever he had the chance. If he had no better reason for being there, he would make a pretense of wiping a grease spot off the shining skin of the plane. Then he would stand by while the young pilot made his preflight check, pulled the canopy shut, and taxied into position with the jet whining sweetly. At the word from the tower he roared down the runway and into the air, a speck in the sky, then gone.

Swallowing his envy, Kirk would turn and hurry back

to work. At least he knew the Sabre was in as perfect mechanical shape as expert care could make it.

"Lieutenant," he asked the young pilot one day, "how's it feel to fly this thing at six hundred miles an hour?"

"Feel, Kayo? Well, mostly I'm too busy to notice much. But there are times—like when you're shooting upstairs after take-off, or leveled out at 35,000 feet on a clear day— you think there's nothing like it on earth. And then," he grinned, "you get other kinds o' feelings. Pulling out of a power dive, for instance. Those G's are pretty rough. When you're on oxygen for a long time, it tires you out, too. Sometimes I get out o' the plane and feel as if I'd hiked ten miles under full pack. Say, why did you ask me? You want to fly a jet yourself?"

Kirk's face reddened, and he turned back to the job he

had been doing. "Sure, sir," he said gruffly. "I'd like to—and I've got about as much chance as a snowball. I had **to** quit college with less than two years."

"Well, gosh, Kayo!" Peabody exclaimed. "I didn't know you felt like that about it. Couldn't you study up—take the exams an' get your credits?"

"I don't know, sir," Kirk replied glumly. "Never tried to find out."

The conversation ended there, but Kirk was still thinking about it when he went back to the barracks that night.

"Hey," one of his flight-mates hailed him. "Mail for you, Kayo."

He took the letter and turned it over, looking at the postmark. It had been mailed in Wichita Falls. When he opened the envelope, he saw a square, boyish handwriting. It was signed by Sergeant Ivar Nelson.

"Dear Kirk," the letter said. "Olga and the kids and I have missed you since you went off to Nevada. I don't write many letters, but I have to tell you I did something after you left. I talked to our personnel officer, Capt. Jenkins. Maybe you remember him. I got him to write to State U., where you went to college. Yesterday he got a letter back, and they say you had pretty good marks up to the time you had to leave. They say they can give full second-year credits in three courses, but you would have to take some examinations in the other two. That would be English History and Mathematics.

"Now, Kirk, maybe you think this was sort of sticking my nose in your business, but I hope you don't take it wrong. We think you would make quite a pilot. If you can find some time to study, I know you could pass those exams, and the college says they'll let you take them right at Nellis whenever you figure you're ready. I would sure like to see you get your chance at flying.

"Let me know how you feel about this. Olga and I would like to think we had helped. She sends you her best."

Kirk turned his back to the room as he finished reading. His eyes were misty, and his hand shook a little when he tried to put the letter back in its envelope. He had no idea how the Air Force would feel about it, but he meant to find out. He couldn't let Sergeant Nelson down after the trouble he'd gone to. It seemed strange that the subject of trying for Aviation Cadet training should have come up twice in less than an hour—almost as if some power outside himself was pushing him in that direction. But for the moment the thing that touched him most was knowing he had a friend as staunch and helpful as the sergeant.

He would have talked to Lieutenant Peabody if he could, but enlisted men weren't allowed over at the Bachelor Officers' Quarters. There was one counselor he could turn to, though—the chaplain. After supper Kirk put on his uniform and made his way to the chaplain's house. He was in and had no visitors at the moment. He knew Kirk from seeing him at chapel. A raw-boned major from Kentucky with several years in the Air Force, he returned the boy's salute, shook his hand, and led the way into his little study.

"Good to see you, Owen," he smiled. "Something on your mind? Sit down and tell me about it."

Haltingly at first, then with more confidence as Major Brown put him at his ease, Kirk told his story. When he finished, the chaplain sat and studied him for a moment, his eyes kind and understanding.

"If you really want to be a Sabre pilot," he said, "and want it hard enough, I have a feeling you'll make it. You know yourself it'll take a lot of work. But there's something else I'll have to tell you. It's true the Air Force needs fliers. But good air mechanics are needed, too. Up to now, you've cost the government several thousand dollars, and they're just beginning to get their investment back. So don't expect the brass to see it your way when you put in an application for Cadet training."

"Aren't there quite a few pilots who started as enlisted men?" Kirk asked, trying not to show his disappointment.

"That's right. Good ones, too. But look at it this way. You're in the last phase of training—beginning to be some use in your job. The Air Force knows you'll make good here. How do they know you've got the tiger blood they want in a jet pilot? You see, not every youngster has it, and it's pretty expensive to find out. Why should the Air Force gamble when they've got a sure thing?"

"I suppose you're right, sir," said Kirk, dejected. "But maybe I'll study for those college credits anyhow. It might help some day to have two full years behind me."

"Just what I was going to suggest," the chaplain agreed

warmly. "My advice would be to tell the Squadron C.O. what you want. The chances are he'll turn you down as a matter of policy, but I'm sure he'll co-operate in letting you take the examinations when you're ready."

Kirk thanked him and went back to the barracks. Before he went to bed, he wrote his mother, asking her to send his textbooks in Trigonometry and English History.

*　　*　　*

Two days later he asked permission to speak to his Squadron Commander Captain Crane. The busy officer looked up from his desk and recognized him.

"At ease, Owen," he said. "Something you want?"

Again Kirk told his story, more briefly this time, because he had rehearsed it carefully. "I'd really like to fly, sir," he finished. "Do you think I could put in an application for transfer to Cadet Training once I've got these credits straightened out?"

The captain frowned a little. His answer was just what the chaplain had led the boy to expect. But at the end he gave Kirk a ray of hope.

"I've no objection to your taking the college exams," he said. "In fact, I'll be glad to help if I can. Then, in a year or so, I'd be more inclined to approve your application. One thing you've got to remember is that fighting planes need two kinds of men—men to fly 'em and men to keep 'em ready to fly. One's just as important as the other. Right now your job is to prove you're a good air mechanic. That's all. Dismissed."

Kirk went back to work. A year seemed like a very long time, but if that was the way it had to be, he was willing to wait.

He had come to Nellis in January. Now, as May drew toward its close, he was beginning to find out what the Nevada climate could provide in the way of heat. At noon the blazing sun sent the temperature well above a hundred, and the men were grateful to be inside the hangars. Still the wind blew dust across the desert, and night and day Kirk could taste the grit in his mouth no matter how much water he drank.

Sergeant Claggett was crustier than ever. He kept them at their tasks, heat or no heat, and when he reprimanded a man for slipshod work, his tongue was like a whiplash. There weren't many occasions for that. They were a good crew, proud of the planes they serviced.

Kirk's friendship with Lieutenant Peabody had continued. He had told the young pilot about the studying he was doing and the captain's promise to consider his application more favorably after a year. When they met in the hangar or on the flight line, Peabody would wink at him and ask how the little cosines were coming or what was the name of Henry the Eighth's third wife.

As a matter of fact, the ruddy-faced young Sabre-jockey was a hero to Kirk. All the glamor of the wild blue yonder seemed to be wrapped up in him. When Kirk worked on Peabody's plane, it was with a special devotion, and he watched his take-offs and landings with admiring eyes. The lieutenant's three months at Nellis were nearly done, and Kirk would hate to see him go.

On a scorching afternoon in early June three flights of F-86's roared off on a gunnery practice mission over the mountains to the north. They were gone nearly two hours— close to their fuel limit—and the hangar crews waited anxiously for the jets to come back. At last they heard the word passed from the tower that the squadron would be landing at 1730 hours. Kirk glanced at the clock and saw it was five-twenty-six. They'd be coming in in four more minutes.

Sergeant Claggett barked an order, and the mechanics

hustled out to the field, each man ready to carry out his special assignment as soon as their planes taxied in. Kirk had an eight-foot ladder of light aluminum, which was used to climb up on the wing.

The first planes were in sight as the crews lined up along the runway. Tiny specks in the sky, they grew larger each second, circling into the pattern, then banking and dropping in a long slant toward the field with flaps and landing gear down.

The wind was gusty and uncertain, and some of the landings were rough. Kirk watched tensely for the wing numbers that would identify their own two jets. At last he saw Peabody's F-86 swooping down and straightening out for the approach.

"Here they come," he yelled, and the words were hardly out of his mouth when Peabody's wheels touched down. The landing was bad, for a sudden gust had tilted the plane at just the wrong instant. The right tire blew out with a bang like a cannon shot, and the jet screamed past dragging a wing tank along the concrete in a shower of sparks and spinning in slow ground loops.

Even before it went by, Kirk was running. There were shouts behind him, and the crash siren was howling from the tower, but he hardly heard them. Ten seconds after the careening plane ground to a stop, he was there, slamming his ladder up against the forward fuselage. As he tugged desperately at the canopy, a blast of heat enveloped him. The fuel in the wing tank was burning with a fierce white flare.

He could see the lieutenant inside, his face ashen and his hands groping feebly for the canopy catch. It came open at last. Kirk reached in and jerked the safety belt free. The flames were so close they were scorching his fatigues, but he put forth all his strength and dragged the pilot out of the cockpit.

By that time the crash wagon and two big red fire trucks had reached the scene. Eager arms caught Peabody as Kirk let go of him. Then Kirk was on the ground and being dragged away from the burning plane. He looked back to see the fire apparatus smother the flames with foam. Then suddenly he was sick. Retching and ashamed, he hung there, supported by the men who held his arms, until the nausea passed.

Kirk was still a little dazed when a young medic steered him to the door of the ambulance.

"Hey!" he expostulated in a choked voice. "What's the idea? Where's the pilot? Where's Lieutenant Peabody?"

"Right here, Kayo," Peabody answered from inside the vehicle. "All in one piece, thanks to you. I guess my head hit something when that tire went out. I was weak as a baby —never would have got clear, I guess. I sure did foul up that landing! What are you in here for?"

"Nothing wrong with me," Kirk told him. "I ought to be reporting back. Claggett won't like it."

"You'll stay right where you are," the medic put in

sharply. "You must be still in shock or you'd feel those burns."

The boy sniffed and caught an odor of charred cloth. Turning his head to the left, he could see black, smoking shreds of uniform on his sleeve and shoulder. Then, for the first time, he felt a wave of searing pain in that area.

"How bad is it?" he asked between clenched teeth.

The ambulance man chuckled. "Not enough for a medical discharge," he said. "You ought to be out and around in three or four days."

They bandaged his burns and put him to bed in the hospital. Peabody had the next cot, but he was up and dressed, lolling in a chair and joking about his mishap.

"How'd you ever get there so quick, Kayo?" he asked. "I bet you ran that hundred yards in under ten flat!"

"I saw the wind tip you," Kirk told him. "Soon as the tire blew, I guess I knew what was going to happen, so I started sprinting. Sure was lucky I lugged that ladder along, though."

"You don't know *how* lucky," said the pilot soberly. "For me, that is. Any little thing I can do for you, Kayo—any time—you just name it."

9

Peabody was only kept in the hospital overnight for observation. Kirk missed him when he was gone, but something had happened to his hero-worship. He knew now that the lieutenant was human and subject to mishaps like other people. On the other hand, he liked him all the better as a friend.

During the four days he was in bed, Kirk got a lot of

studying done. His burns were painful but not too deep. He felt them most when the dressings were changed. The rest of the time he was able to concentrate on his books and mathematical problems. In writing to his mother, he didn't even mention the accident to Peabody's plane. The news would only have worried her.

On the third day Major Brown dropped in to see him. The big Kentuckian was interested in the studying he was doing and helped him with a couple of questions in Trigonometry.

"I thought I was going to be an engineer once," he explained. "Took a lot of math before I decided on the ministry. But I reckon the Lord can find a use for everything I've studied."

As he got up to leave, the chaplain gripped Kirk's hand hard. "You remember what I said the other night," he asked, "about the Air Force needing pilots with tiger blood? Well, Owen, after what you did out there on the field, I don't think they'll have to look much farther. So long, my boy, and good luck!"

They took Kirk's bandages off after five days, and on the sixth he went back to the barracks and to work. Sergeant Claggett greeted him in the hangar with poker-faced grimness.

"About time you showed up around here," he growled. "The lieutenant's got a new airplane to take the place o' the one that burned. An' he don't want any mechanic to work on it but you. I have to say you turned in a pretty fair job the other day. Only next time you better wait for an order."

Kirk worked happily all morning. His back and arm were still a bit sore, but they bothered him no more than a bad case of sunburn. When he marched back with the crew to noon chow, an Airman, First Class, hailed him.

"Cap'n Crane wants you to report," he told Kirk. "Yeah, right now. Come as you are."

He entered the captain's office and saluted.

"Sit down, Owen," the officer said. "How are you feeling by now?"

"First class, sir. They fixed me up fine."

"Good. I won't keep you but a minute. Lieutenant Peabody seems to think quite a bit of you, and he asked me a favor. Are you still as keen as ever to be an Aviation Cadet?"

"Yes, *sir!*" Kirk replied eagerly.

"Think you're ready to pass the college tests?"

"I—I guess so, sir."

"All right. They're here in my desk. The chaplain—he's another friend of yours, by the way—has offered to proctor the exams Saturday. You'll be relieved from duty so you can take them. Report to Major Brown Saturday morning at 0800."

Kirk got up. Apparently he was dismissed, but he had a question he must ask.

"Sir," he blurted, "do you mean—if I get through the exams—you'll approve my cadet application?"

The captain's eyes twinkled. "Let's take things one at a time," he said. "Your first job is to hit the exams and hit 'em hard."

At eight o'clock on Saturday morning Kirk knocked on the chaplain's door. And at four that afternoon he left, brain-weary but happy. The two three-hour tests hadn't been too hard. He felt pretty sure he had passed them both—certainly the one in Mathematics. There had been a couple of tricky questions in English History, but he thought he'd given the right answers. Anyhow, he'd find out soon. Captain Crane had promised to mail the papers that night.

He waited with what patience he could muster through

the week end, Monday, Tuesday, and Wednesday. On Thursday morning he was called into the captain's office once more.

Crane was smiling. He held out a piece of printed paper.

"Here's the application form for Aviation Cadets," he said. "You came through the exams with flying colors, and I have your college credits to attach to the application."

Kirk had to sit down for a minute before his hand stopped shaking. Then he took a pen and filled in the form. Before he left, he saw the captain mark it approved and put it in the mail.

He still had a month to wait before the examining team came through Nellis. It wasn't easy, but he buckled down to his job and learned all he could about the mechanical workings of the F-86. Sergeant Claggett growled at the prospect of losing him. It was obvious, however, that he held no real resentment. He saw to it that the young mechanic had no time for daydreaming and gave him as much instruction as ever.

Kirk didn't see much of Lieutenant Peabody, for the squadron was finishing its gunnery course and preparing to leave. On the last day the young fighter pilot came around to say good-by. He shook hands with each member of Claggett's crew. Last of all he came to Kirk.

"Got a feeling I'll be seeing you again, Kayo," he grinned. "We're taking off for Japan and then Korea. Get those wings in a hurry and come on over."

There were a dozen or more candidates for cadet training assembled in the Flight dayroom the morning the examining team arrived. Each man was put through a long series of searching questions and had his military record carefully studied. Then came a thorough physical check. When it was all over, there were only eight men accepted, and Kirk was one of them.

The captain called him in that night and congratulated him.

"You've been in the Air Force a year, Owen," he said. "Sometimes I think every officer ought to have that experience as an enlisted man. Believe me, it wasn't a year wasted. You'll not only make a better Aviation Cadet because of it, but you'll know more about the planes you fly."

He took a paper from his desk and checked a list typed on it. "You're assigned to Marana for Primary," he said. "That's a civilian contract school down near Tucson. Good place, they tell me. The new class starts in a week."

Kirk nodded. "There's just one thing, sir," he said. "I haven't been home since the day I enlisted, and I haven't had any leave. Suppose I could get a few days?"

"Good idea," the captain agreed. "You can go tomorrow, and I'll try to get you on an eastbound plane for part of the trip."

The boy packed his duffel, thrilled by the day's developments. He started to send a wire home, then decided to surprise his family. Before 0800 next morning he was aboard a B-29 bomber headed for Kansas City.

Early in the afternoon he was lucky enough to get a second ride on an Air Force C-47 that landed him at Jennison Field—on the very airstrip where he and his friends had raced their hot rods. It was easy to hitch a ride to Clarksdale, and just before suppertime he swung up the street, whistling the Air Force song loud and clear.

Margie was on the front porch. "Mother!" she screamed. "Come quick—it's Kirk!"

*   *   *

Six days later Cadet Owen reported for duty at Marana Air Base. It was a pretty place, he thought. There were palm trees and flowering cactus, and the dry Arizona heat was

tempered by winds off the Tortolita Mountains. But before
he had time to do more than glance at the scenery, he was
involved in the stiff schedule of Primary Flying School.

First came the processing—very much like what he had
gone through at Lackland. Here his experience was valu-
able, for he was able to help steer the bewildered young
civilians and even the Air R.O.T.C. boys through the maze
of detail. A really rugged physical examination weeded out
nearly 10 per cent of the cadet candidates. Along with it
came the close-cropped haircuts, the talks with the chaplain,
and all the rest. Then they were issued their uniforms. On
the khaki blouses were shoulder boards of dark blue—the
distinguishing marks of the Aviation Cadet.

The first month of the course was Preflight Training, and
it was the toughest routine Kirk had found in the Air Force.
Only the fact that the youngsters were athletes in superb
condition prevented many of them from dropping out. There
were hours of marching and physical drill in the blazing
heat, more hours of ground-school work, and the constant,
rigorous discipline imposed by the upperclassmen.

Kirk was gladder than ever that he had been through the
mill the year before. His rating as an Airman, Third, meant
nothing now. He was back at the bottom rung of the ladder,
often reminded by cadets who had graduated from Preflight that he was the lowest form of life. Yet much of his
previous training gave him an edge over his mates. He knew
how to march, to make a bed, and to keep his equipment
ready for white-glove inspections, of which there were
many.

Rigid rules governed the conduct of the beginners. All
of them were called by one name—"Mister." When they
went from field to classroom, they had to turn square corners. In the mess hall they ate "square meals"—sitting stiffly
erect and making right-angled motions when they put food

in their mouths. Frequently they were ordered to stand at attention, stomachs and chins in, chests out, hands straight down at their sides.

It was tough, but it was necessary. There was no place for weaklings among the men who were to fly. In the first three weeks more than 10 per cent of the cadets were found unable to take it and were sent elsewhere.

In one way Kirk was behind some of his class. He had never piloted any type of airplane, and he soon discovered that a lot of the others were experts. At least, that was the impression he got from hearing them talk. Some of the men from R.O.T.C. colleges had been given training in Piper Cubs. Others—quite a number, in fact—had flown small aircraft with the Civil Air Patrol.

Whitey Collins was one of this group. He was a strapping, six-foot farm boy from western Nebraska, and his bed stood next to Kirk's.

"Wait till they start us flyin'," he said frequently. "I'll show these ground-poundin' officers! Why, we own three ranches at home—all a hundred miles apart. Some days I've got in the Piper Tripacer an' flown to all three places in one afternoon. Better'n a hundred hours I've had in that plane."

When Kirk had heard about it for the tenth time, he began to wonder just how good Whitey would turn out to be. A Tripacer was a nice little airplane, and he envied anybody who owned one. But from all he heard—and the Preflight trainees talked about little else—they'd start their flying in T-6's. The T-6 was different—bigger, faster, and "hotter" in every way. Maybe the light-plane pilots wouldn't have such an edge after all.

The courses they studied during their month of ground school were largely familiar to Kirk. Aircraft science and engineering was one in which he knew about as much as the instructors, though he tried not to show it. Others, in which he had had some earlier classes, dealt with leadership, military intelligence, and Air Force organization. Finally, because they were in training to become officers and gentlemen, they were drilled in customs and courtesies and the Honor Code.

There were two inspections each day—really tough inspections, where a wrinkle or a smudge would bring a demerit, commonly known as a "gig." During Preflight each man was limited to ten gigs a week. After they started flying, the number allowed would be cut to six. When a man drew too many gigs, he had to walk tours, and so there were always a few cadets marching stiffly in front of their quarters while the others read, studied, or played ball.

At full-dress Retreat parade, on one of their first afternoons in ground school, the colonel in command of the base explained to them that they were now entering the fourth class.

"You'll advance from one class to the next every six weeks," he told them. "As fourth classmen you will be restricted to the base at all times. The third class will be allowed occasional week-end open post. The second class will have unrestricted week-end open post. And when you reach the first class, you will have open post one night a week as well as week ends."

The day they were promoted to third-class status it was announced that one out of three men would get a Saturday pass. After their weeks of confinement to the base it was an important occasion.

A lieutenant read off names slowly from a long list, and as each man answered he took one pace forward.

Kirk stood there sweating in the afternoon heat, his shoulders squared, his eyes to the front. A lot of names were called while he waited. At last the tension broke. "Owen,

K," barked the lieutenant, and the boy stepped forward. He had made the select group.

One of Kirk's close friends was a slim, black-haired young Detroiter named Ron MacLean. He had a little money from home and invited Kirk to go with him to Tucson.

When they left the base that afternoon, feeling extra smart in their new uniforms, there were some envious glances cast their way by cadets who had been less fortunate. Whitey Collins was one of them. He had drawn a lot of gigs for sloppiness and for arguing back at upperclassmen. Now he scowled resentfully at Kirk and Ron as they went by.

"I don't think Whitey likes this deal," Kirk chuckled.

"You mean 'three-ranch Tripacer' Collins?" said Ron. "No. 'Fraid not. I bet he's saying 'wait till we get to flying' right now."

"You've had some light-plane time," Kirk remarked. "Think it'll make much difference?"

"Sure, it ought to help the first week or two. After that I imagine we'll all level out about the same."

Tucson was swarming with the blue uniforms of officers and airmen, for a bomber base—Davis-Monthan—was located close by.

The two boys did the town in leisurely fashion, took in a movie, and went to dinner at a lovely, rambling, modern-style hotel. For a while they debated taking a room there for the night, but the cheapest one available was fifteen dollars, and Ron's Scotch instincts prevailed. However, they had the luxury of lolling in bed next morning in their barracks and going for a swim in the pool in the afternoon. That night Kirk had a hard time getting to sleep. Tomorrow he would start Flight Training!

10

The first two days were spent getting acquainted with the T-6. It looked pretty formidable to Kirk when he stood beside it listening to the briefing. It was high off the ground, with a barrel-chested fuselage and a big radial engine in front. The canopy over the two-place cockpit was less streamlined than those of the jets, but the plane looked like business, rugged and stoutly built. The number of instruments on the panel made Kirk realize that this was no play-toy he would be learning to fly.

He spent most of the second day memorizing those instruments and their functions. In the evening he and Ron went through the check-out procedure over and over, till they were letter-perfect. And on the third day Kirk went up for the first time.

The instructor was a soft-spoken, quiet civilian from Colorado. He had been a Mustang pilot in the war and later in the Air National Guard, and his sure mastery of the plane made Kirk feel at ease. They strapped themselves in, checked the T-6 out, started the engine, taxied to the head of the runway, and revved up. The take-off run was fast, and Kirk watched the shortening strip ahead with his heart in his mouth. Then the plane jumped into the air, and he breathed more easily. The landing gear was retracted, and with the stick well back they climbed to 4,000 feet. There the instructor leveled off. Half a dozen other trainers were in the sky, and they flew a prescribed course to keep clear of them. After ten minutes they circled into the pattern, checked with the tower, and came in for the landing when their turn arrived. On this first flight Kirk had been told to keep his hands on the dual controls, so as to get the feel of it while the pilot did the actual flying from the rear seat.

Comparing notes with his friend MacLean, he learned that Ron had taken over the controls during part of his flight. "But," the other boy told him, "I've still got a couple o' weeks of dual before I can solo. Don't worry, Kayo. You'll catch up."

The primary course called for 130 hours of flying. That meant each man was up two and sometimes three times a day. Before the end of the week, Kirk was flying the T-6 regularly while they were in the air. He had good co-ordination, and he quickly learned how the plane responded to the controls. Consciously he tried to copy the light, sure touch of his instructor.

There was no time for daydreaming in the air. He was thinking every second, watching the instruments, checking air speed and wind drift, keeping an eye on the landmarks below. A lot of it, he knew, would become instinctive after enough practice, but until then he had to concentrate on his job.

His first take-off and landing came sooner than he had expected.

"All right, Mister," the Colorado man told him with a grin. "I'm just a passenger this trip. She's yours."

Kirk drew a deep breath. His mind went over the procedure without panic. He knew he was ready. Yet five minutes later, roaring down the runway, there was a fleeting instant when everything seemed unreal. He waited as long as he dared and pulled back on the stick, knowing as he did so that it was too soon and too hard. Luckily the T-6 didn't stall out. She climbed drunkenly, then gathered enough power to clear the buildings at the end of the field. He got the wheels up, retracted the flaps, and leveled out on course.

"Now you know," said the voice from the rear seat, "why instructors have gray hairs. You'll do better next time. What you did was normal for beginners."

Strangely enough, the landing, which had worried Kirk much more than the take-off, was accomplished without trouble. He came in at just the right altitude, and his glide path was perfect. There was scarcely a jolt as the wheels touched.

"Smooth as butter," said the instructor approvingly.

There were other landings, many of them, as the days went by. Kirk found out he had been very lucky on that first one. The T-6 was a fairly hot plane to land, mushy on the controls if the approach speed was too low. He managed to avoid accidents, but some of his landings were of the kangaroo type—a series of bouncy jumps. With practice his average got better, and he was having no more trouble with take-offs.

Not all the cadets came through without accidents, and some of the worst ones happened to men who had flown light planes. Kirk was in the flight pattern one afternoon when Whitey Collins went in to land just ahead of him. The T-6 wasn't quite level, and the left wing dipped, hitting the runway after the wheels touched down. There was a scream of grinding metal as the plane ground-looped, and crash cars raced out with sirens howling.

In his earphones Kirk heard the "no landing" warning from the tower. He pulled back on the stick and felt the instructor in the rear seat take over the controls. The engine revved up to full throttle with a roar. They pulled out of their glide, climbed, and went back into the pattern until the damaged plane was hauled off the runway.

Fortunately nobody was seriously hurt. Ron MacLean had a theory about what had happened.

"You probably wouldn't notice," he told Kirk, "but the landing wheels on a T-6 are closer together than on a Cub, for instance, or a Tripacer. That narrow gear makes it a lot easier to ground-loop if you come in with one wing low. Whitey must have thought he was flying his dad's plane back on the ranch."

It was a lesson Kirk didn't forget. He was always careful to keep his wings level when he landed.

Graduation from Preflight had brought no relaxation in drill or inspections. But by this time most of the cadets had become accustomed to the discipline. They marched everywhere—to classes, to chow, and to the flight line. The ranks were straight, and they kept in step. As they marched, they sang—tunes with a good swing to them, like "Jolly, Jolly Sixpence" and "Yellow Ribbon." Some of these young men had been pretty sloppy citizens when they came to Marana. Now they carried themselves like officers, even though they had a long way to go.

The 130 hours flying time scheduled for Primary included both dual and solo. But a lot of their experience came from the additional twenty hours they logged in Link Trainers. Kirk was sure he never would have learned to fly on instruments without the time he put in in the Links. They were ingenious devices housed in a hangar. Each one was a perfect replica of a plane cockpit, complete with instruments and controls. And in response to the cadets' actions they tilted forward or back, banked for turns—even went into a spin if mishandled.

The instructor was able to talk to the student over the intercom while he "flew" the Link. There were classic stories of cadets who were told after ten minutes struggling with a flight problem, "You are now 120 degrees off course, flying upside down. Your altitude is 1,000 feet *underground*."

Kirk never quite got himself into such a predicament, but he did make mistakes and learned how to correct them.

The day of his first real solo flight dawned clear and hot. There was very little breeze. He tested it nervously with a wetted finger and knew he would have a long take-off run. The instructor checked him out on the flight line and grinned at his worried look.

"You're lucky there's no crosswind," he told the boy. "Just be sure you've got plenty of ground speed and up you'll go. Take her out ten miles or so—say five minutes— then make your 180-degree turn and come back into the pattern. Stay at 4,000."

Kirk adjusted his radio phones, felt his parachute harness and seat belt, then signaled the crew to start the engine. Evidently they knew in the tower that he was a first-solo man. The instructions came over smooth and loud. When he had warmed up the engine, he taxied out to the end of the field and went through his final check procedure. Then he heard the encouraging voice again.

"Okay, four-eight-two. You are cleared for take-off. Good luck!"

"Four-eight-two to tower," he answered. "Roger. And thanks!"

Releasing the brakes, he eased into position on the runway and slowly pushed the throttle forward. Gradually picking up speed, he began to feel the plane respond to the pressure on the rudder pedals as he strove to keep it centered on the runway. Faster and faster the concrete went by. No wind. He'd need a little extra distance. When the plane began to feel light and ready to fly, he gave it two seconds more, then eased back on the stick. The T-6 lifted smoothly, and he was air-borne. He retracted the landing gear and went on up. As he watched the altimeter climb, he inhaled a great lungful of air. Only then did he realize he had been holding his breath during the last thousand feet of run.

A tremendous feeling of exhilaration took hold of him. Here he was—all alone—master of the sky. No matter what other craft he might fly in the future, this was an unforgettable moment.

Coming back to reality, he checked the time, the compass, and the altitude. His air speed was close to 190, and he was still on course. At the end of five minutes he banked to the left, made his turn, and headed back to the field.

As he entered the pattern, he began concentrating on his landing.

"Marana tower," he called into the microphone, "this is Air Force four-eight-two on the base leg, wheels down and locked. Over."

"Roger, four-eight-two, you are cleared for the final," the towerman replied.

Approaching the field, Kirk tried to gauge his altitude above the end of the runway. For an anxious moment he was afraid he might land short of the concrete. He had to fight off the temptation to pull back on the stick, even though he knew this would slow his glide and make the airplane mush to the ground faster. At last the runway markers sped past, and he realized he was actually a little higher than he should be. Tensely he pulled into his flare-out. The T-6 lost flying speed and settled with a solid thump on the runway. As he taxied back to his waiting instructor, he relaxed with a sigh of relief and satisfaction.

In September cadet officers were appointed to command units in the military organization of the base. Achievement and qualities of leadership were the factors that counted most. When Kirk was made a squadron captain, the honor caught him completely off guard. He was dazed when the Commandant of Cadets called him out of formation and gave him the four-barred epaulettes that symbolized his new rank.

With the title went some added responsibility. He had to enforce cadet discipline in the squadron and issue orders to his two flight lieutenants, one of whom was Ron MacLean. Kirk didn't let it go to his head. He realized that the rank was temporary—"just playing soldier," as the disgruntled Whitey Collins put it. But he took a justifiable pride in the fact that so far, at least, he had made good.

He wrote a letter home and another to Ginnie Gordon, signing his name with a flourish—"Kirk Owen, Cadet Captain, U.S.A.F."

Early in the fall they got their first experience of night flying. It wasn't too difficult, for the Arizona nights were clear, and even by starlight it was possible to identify geographical landmarks. Night landings were the only things that bothered Kirk, and he soon learned to judge heights and distances.

Next came twenty hours of instrument flying. Here he found the Link Trainer had given him confidence. He wasn't afraid to come in blind, trusting the dials on the instrument panel, even when his senses told him they were wrong.

In the final phases of the course, the cadets got eight hours of acrobatics and eight hours of navigation. They had already learned how to fly in tight formation, with wingtips only a couple of yards apart. Now they were schooled in precision snap rolls, slow rolls, and loops.

The first time Kirk saw the Arizona landscape stretching out over his head he had a queer feeling. Then he got used to it. The plane handled well upside-down, and as long as he had plenty of altitude and air speed, everything was fine. He learned to trust the needle-ball and air-speed indicator instead of his own instinctive reactions. Flying under instrument conditions, his instinct was likely to be wrong by twenty to forty degrees.

Navigation was a matter of mathematics and accuracy. Judgment was involved only as far as the checking of figures was concerned. Some of the students didn't believe the computations or made the same mistake time after time. As a result they got hopelessly off course. The final check ride on navigation resulted in washing out several of the remaining cadets. Others had already gone because of poor instrument flying or general lack of progress.

Looking over the lists, Kirk realized that nearly 35 per cent of those who had started Primary had fallen by the wayside. At the same time he knew that the ones who remained were good. The men had been separated from the boys.

The streets of Tucson were decorated for Christmas when their training at Marana drew to a close. Kirk had been in the Air Force nearly a year and a half, but he felt now that he was on his way. The Korean fighting still went on, bitter and without decision. But at least one part of the news was good. The F-86 fighters were knocking down MIG-15's. Maybe he could still get there in time to help.

At the time of graduation from Primary each cadet was given a chance to state his choice of single-engine or multi-engine flying. That didn't mean he would get what he asked for. The decision was based on the instructor's rating first and the student's request second. Kirk had no doubts about what he wanted. He chose single-engine and hoped for the best.

His instructor must have agreed that he had the makings of a fighter pilot, for when the lists were posted next day Kirk was named for basic single-engine training at Williams AFB.

*   *   *

A month before, Kirk had bought his modest Christmas gifts and mailed them. Just as he was leaving Marana, a small battered package arrived. It was from Ginnie—a little figure of a flying bird carved in ivory. He didn't know much about oriental art, but he knew that this was rare and beautiful. Somewhere in Japan—for that was where she was stationed now—she must have found it in a bazaar. He had written her that he was flying now, and the little ivory bird was a symbol. It made him a little ashamed of the service-weight nylon stockings he had sent her on the advice of the clerk in the Marana store.

He didn't have to hitch a plane ride to his new base. Williams was not far from Phoenix—only about seventy miles up the highway from Marana. He and his fellow cadets traveled by bus.

Hundreds of men from other Basic schools were moving in at the same time, for Williams was a big place—one of the principal Basic Training bases for single-engine pilots. All of them started on an equal footing. Cadet officer rank and honors were left behind, and each man had his own way to make. Their uniforms remained the same, but they were issued new shoulder bars with the stripes running lengthwise instead of across.

Ron MacLean had been posted for Williams, too, and by staying together, they managed to be assigned to the same Flight.

The first week was taken up with processing and ground school. They listened with keen attention now to the lectures on jet air tactics. Kirk realized, his spine atingle, that everything he learned about fighting MIG's was serious business—possibly a matter of life and death. And there was plenty of good information available. Many of the instructors were men who had returned from Korea and knew from experience what jet dog-fighting was like.

The courses they were given included Aircraft Science, Mathematics, Military Law, Flight Planning, Public Speaking, Jet Navigation, and Weather. After the first week they would combine ground school with flight time, alternating morning and afternoon sessions. There were physical training periods three times a week, and wherever they went, they marched.

The six months of Basic Flight Training gave them 120 hours of flying, dual and solo. Kirk found the T-28 very much like the T-6—just bigger, faster, and a bit more complicated. The main difference was in the tricycle landing gear, which called for a slightly different landing procedure. He mastered it in his first few dual flights and was ready to solo before the first month ended.

Like all the other cadets, Kirk was eager to get into the jet phase of training. He saw the T-33's taking off, heard the high whine of their engines, and could hardly wait for the day when he would fly one.

Meanwhile, his class had to go through physiological tests and learn how to use both "demand" and "pressure" oxygen systems. They would be flying at very high altitudes when they got into fighters, and sudden decompression of the cockpit would be a hazard. So, in small groups they were put through the decompression chamber. It was a ground installation built to simulate a pressurized cockpit. In a few seconds the atmospheric pressure could be dropped to the equivalent of the thin air at 36,000 feet—just as if a cannon shell had shattered the plane. It was a rough experience, and some of the men blacked out.

Oxygen was a vital factor in high-altitude flight. In the demand system, the pilot had to breathe the oxygen in. The pressure system, used for jet flying, forced it into his lungs. One thing they all had to do was get used to wearing oxygen masks.

At last they completed their seventy hours of time in the T-28's and were ready for the "T-birds," as the T-33's were affectionately called.

Actually it wasn't as thrillingly different as Kirk had expected. The T-bird handled very much like the T-28, though its top speed was about two hundred miles an hour higher. Still, he felt it marked a forward step toward his goal, and he set himself to learn everything about jet flying that the T-33 could teach him.

Any jet engine worked more efficiently at high altitudes. Nearer the ground it was a fuel hog. So the trick was to climb fast to 20,000 feet and stay that high through most of the training flight. Another difference was in the instrument panel. All throttle settings were based on the RPM gauge, which showed the per cent of maximum revolutions per minute turned up by the turbo. At 90 per cent RPM, the engine would be delivering about 75 per cent of maximum thrust.

Other new instruments were the Mach indicator—which was a separate, striped needle on the air-speed gauge—and

USAF

a tail-pipe temperature gauge. Most of the rest were familiar.

Kirk had a Korean veteran as an instructor. He was a weather-beaten man of thirty-five, who had been a pilot since the middle of World War II. He didn't talk much, but what he said was worth listening to because it dealt largely with Sabrejet flying.

"Can't afford to make any mistakes coming in to land," he would say. "If you've taken a hit, don't let down for the field approach unless you're dead sure you can make it. You can't pick up power for another go-round when you're at low altitude. Up in the sky these jets are wonderful. At slow speed an' low they're dogs."

There were nine hours of instrument flying in the T-bird. They did some tight formation flying, too, and plenty of acrobatics. Gunnery practice, air to ground, was among the last phases of their instruction. By this time, Kirk had no doubts about his ability to fly a jet airplane. He wasn't cocky. He just never thought about it. Concentrating on the job, he had reached the point where doing the right thing at the right instant was a habit.

When it came to firing at ground targets, the same good eyes and sharp reflexes that had brought him top scores with a carbine gave him an edge over most of his fellow students.

From the time they had first reached Williams, they had heard about the "boom bucket." It was a tall, slanting steel tower, braced with tripod legs, that stood by itself off in a corner of the base.

Now, in the last weeks of training, each man got a closer introduction to it.

"This," said the instructor to the waiting file of cadets, "is an ejection seat tower—the only one at any training base in the Air Force. It operates exactly the way your ejection seat will work in an F-86. You'll want to know the feel of it in case you ever have to pop yourself out of a Sabre."

One after another they were strapped into the seat, feet in the stirrups, arms in the arm rests, and head held stiffly erect against the head rest. A catapult and explosive cartridge shot the seat upward when the student pressed the trigger.

Kirk's turn came early. He climbed in, tightened the seat belt and shoulder straps, and braced himself for the jolt of the ejection. Under his right forefinger, in the bend of the arm rest, he could feel the trigger. He drew a deep breath and squeezed it. *Whoosh!*

He had wondered what fifteen "G's" would feel like. That, he knew, was the force of gravity encountered in the first nine or ten feet of rise, when the seat was going up at sixty feet a second. But as he came to a stop, forty feet up the tower, he realized it hadn't hurt at all. His mouth must have flown open, for there he sat, grinning like a jack-o'-lantern. Otherwise there was just nothing to it. He unhooked the seat belt at once—as he would have to do if ejected from a plane. When he was lowered to the ground, he got out, still grinning. He knew then that if the time should ever come when he had to blast out of a falling jet, he could do it with confidence.

11

The dry, fierce heat of June was over Arizona when graduation time approached. Kirk had been almost too busy to notice his surroundings at Williams, but on the last day or two he had a little free time. With Ron MacLean he borrowed a jeep from a friend in town, and they explored the Valley of the Sun, where the big base was located.

To the westward lay miles of flat, irrigated farm land, bordered by the sagebrush of the desert. Onions, melons, and oranges grew there the year 'round, tended by Mexican laborers, and there were roadside stands loaded with fruit and vegetables along the highways.

They drove east toward the high ramparts of the Superstition Mountains. A road led up through the foothills, and they found the air growing cooler as they climbed. Then a rough trail branched off along the floor of a canyon. On an impulse they turned off, trusting the jeep to make its way up the rocky track. The canyon walls cut off the sun, and the temperature dropped ten degrees in the shadow.

"Maybe the lost Dutchman's gold strike's up this trail," said Ron idly. "I hear there've been prospectors hunting it for fifty years. Supposed to be the richest mine in the whole of Arizona."

Kirk chuckled. "I doubt if a couple o' tenderfeet like us are going to find it then," he said. "Besides, even a jeep can't get much farther. Look at those boulders ahead."

He stopped the little car in a fairly level spot, wide enough to turn around with some backing and filling. And just at that moment coming down the trail they heard a clop-clop of hoofs.

"Speak o' the devil!" Ron murmured. "Look at that—a prospector!"

An old, bearded man in a sweat-blackened sombrero came slouching around a rocky bend. Behind him was a burro carrying a heavy pack. The man came to a halt, staring at the jeep and at their uniforms through red-rimmed, watery eyes. Finally he opened his mouth.

" 'Tain't goin' to do you no good," he croaked. "Look all

you please, but you'll never find it. Why? 'Cause I found it—y'ars ago. Cleaned it out. Here's all that's left."

He fumbled in a pocket of his threadbare jeans and pulled out a small, gleaming nugget. "Yep," he said. "All that's left o' the Dutchman's gold. I sure had one wallopin' bender, though, 'fore it was spent!"

With a toothless grin he went shambling off, the patient little gray beast following obediently at his heels.

"Well," Ron laughed, "there's the mystery o' the Dutchman's mine, all solved an' settled."

"Maybe," said Kirk. "Seemed to me he was mighty anxious to keep us from going any farther. But we've got more important things to do than worrying about lost gold mines. We'd better be starting back."

Graduation from Basic was a big event in cadet training. The main ceremony came at Retreat formation, after the heat of the day was gone. For an hour they stood at attention. A grizzled major general with six rows of ribbons made a short, strong speech about the tradition they were inheriting. Then, in rapid succession, each man was given his second lieutenant's bars, and the silver wings of the Air Force pilot were pinned above the left breast pocket of his tunic.

Kirk was trembling when it was over. He felt exalted, prouder than he had ever been in all his life. There was a big, hilarious party at the Officers' Club that night, but he got there late. He had taken time to write three letters—to Ivar Nelson, who had helped to make it possible, to his family, and to Ginnie Gordon.

*   *   *

Two days later he was back at Nellis AFB in Las Vegas. The whole class of newly graduated pilots from Williams moved in at the same time. There was no lost motion once they arrived. This was the "finishing school" for Sabrejet fighters, and the need for them was great.

They were processed rapidly in one building, where the Flight Surgeon, Finance Officer, Chaplain, and other interested parties took them in turn. The briefings were short and to the point. No long, involved explanations were necessary, for cadet graduates were accepted as intelligent officers. At the end of the processing they were assigned to squadrons with numbers and picturesque names—Bulldogs, Bobcats, Jayhawks, and the like. Kirk and Ron both found themselves assigned to the Jayhawks of Squadron 379T.

Each man received a sheaf of papers, including questionnaires, handbooks, and information covering the instruments in the F-86. Ground school started the morning after they arrived, and ground classes alternated with flying. They began studying such vital subjects as F-86 engineering, Air Force intelligence, and the best ways to survive if they were shot down over hostile territory.

Some of the young second lieutenants laughed at the lectures on survival. Kirk wasn't one of them. He had enough imagination to feel the lonely despair of a man—wounded, perhaps, and far behind the lines—who faced the stark choice of escape or capture by a barbarous enemy. Of course, it wasn't likely to happen to him. But if it should, he wanted to know all he could about staying alive and free.

On the second day they assembled at the squadron operations building with helmets, parachutes, G-suits, and other gear they had been issued. Marching out to the flight line, they were introduced to those sleek, incredibly fast terrors of the sky, the F-86 Sabrejets. The briefing was long and intensive. In small groups of half a dozen men they were given every detail of the planes they would be flying. Once more Kirk was inwardly grateful for the months he had put in as an F-86 mechanic. He knew things about the plane and its construction that few of the rest would ever learn.

The Sabre was a one-place airplane. There was no room for an instructor, ready to take the controls if a student got in trouble. You had to fly it alone, from scratch. Kirk had known this for a long time, and sometimes he had lain awake nights worrying about it. Yet now that he was face to face with his first Sabre solo, he wasn't afraid.

It wasn't that he was overconfident of his own ability. But he was pretty sure he could fly as well as the average in his class. Also, he had concentrated on every word of briefing, and the words were firmly imbedded in his mind.

His instructor for this all-important first flight was a lean young first lieutenant from Oregon. He had flown seventy missions over Korea and had two MIG's and a probable third to his credit. Hospitalized home after a bout of pneumonia, he had been assigned to Nellis after his recovery.

"I've read your training record, Owen," he said. "You'll do all right. Just remember you've got a very hot airplane under you, and until you're accustomed to it you'd better do just what I tell you. This is a chase ride. I'll be right on your tail all the way, talking to you. Give her full RPM on the take-off and go up to 20,000, course southwest, 240 degrees. I'll be there to tell you what to do next."

Without hurry Kirk went through the check routine he had learned so carefully. The instructor, Lieutenant Corliss, stood on the cockpit ladder till it was completed, then climbed down. "Okay," he grinned, and made a circle sign with his thumb and forefinger.

The starter cart fired up Kirk's jet. It took hold smoothly with a low moan that rose rapidly in pitch. He waited till he heard Corliss's voice in his earphones.

"Jayhawk Trout Two to tower," the lieutenant said. "Request take-off clearance for two."

The name "Trout" was the Flight designation. Each of the Flights in Jayhawk Squadron was named for a fish. "Two" meant that Corliss was flying wing.

The tower replied that the request was granted and named the runway they were to use. Kirk had already closed the canopy. Now he released the brakes and moved out, taxiing slowly on reduced power. The other F-86 followed close behind him.

At the head of the runway he paused, revved up the engine till the plane quivered.

"All right, Owen," came the instructor's calm voice. "Take her away."

There was no sudden rush. The jet seemed to gather speed slowly but steadily. After a mile he had the RPM gauge up to 95 per cent and was moving so fast the field was a blur.

"You've got it," said Corliss. "Ease her back."

He pulled gently on the stick and felt himself instantly air-borne. Quickly he retracted the gear. Then in a flash he was at 200 feet and climbing—climbing faster than ever before. He checked his course and watched the altimeter needle. Five thousand—ten thousand—fifteen—all in what seemed like a few seconds. Below him was the desert. Las Vegas was a cluster of white dots. The mountains looked like brown windrows of hay.

"I'm right with you, kid," said Corliss. "At 20,000 cut your RPM a little and level off. Back to 90 per cent. Now let's see a couple of chandelles. From the right side first."

The chandelle was a maneuver Kirk had learned long ago. It was simple enough, but you had to fly it all the way. It gave you the feel of an airplane and what it could do.

He pulled the stick back and climbed at a steep angle— nearly eighty degrees. Then he lifted the right wing high and came over into a dive, with the far-off ground rushing toward him.

"Pretty good," he heard the instructor say. "But you didn't use all you had. Don't be afraid of it. This time go up till she starts to feel just a bit mushy."

He pulled out of the dive at better than 650 an hour and started to climb again. Up—up—almost vertically. At 25,000 he knew from the feel of the controls that the plane was nearing a stall. But he was still able to bank to the left and start his dive.

"That's better," Corliss told him. "See what I mean? Now let's see some lazy eights."

Kirk caught a glimpse of the other Sabre off his right wing as he lifted again. The lazy eights were simply more chandelles done in opposite directions, first to the left, then to the right. When they were completed to the instructor's satisfaction, he told Kirk to pull back on the stick for a fast climb and try a high speed stall at 25,000 feet.

With all that altitude a stall was safe enough, and Kirk got the feel of the airplane as it slammed upward to a sudden stop and started to fall. Other experiments followed, till he knew the capabilities of the Sabre under all kinds of stall conditions. He had been up more than twenty minutes now, and the gauge showed a little over half his fuel remained.

"Head east for about two minutes," Corliss told him. "You'll see a dry lake down below Boulder City. There's a road running down the middle, and I want you to pretend it's a landing strip. You're to suppose that runway is at 15,000 feet. Come down to 16,000 and practice a landing—dive, wing flaps, and wheels down—the works. We'll fly the down-wind leg and come around, just as if we were back at the base."

Kirk spotted the dry lake bottom and the road. He swung ninety degrees left and flew downwind for half a minute. Then, at the instructor's order, he took another short leg westward and turned into the wind on the approach leg. It seemed strange to go through the landing procedure at that high altitude, but it was good practice, even to the final stall that would have put him on the ground.

"Good!" Corliss called. "Now gun her and bring her round again. Wheels up!"

The engine took hold well at 15,000 feet. In a moment he had it up to 90 RPM and the lake had vanished behind him.

Twice more Corliss had him go through the maneuver, polishing his technique. "All right," said the instructor. "Let's go home and see how it works on a real strip."

They boomed along on a northward course and cut into the pattern a few miles south of Nellis.

Corliss called the tower. "Jayhawk Trout Two entering downwind leg with two."

He continued talking Kirk in. Their flaps and wheels were down as they swung into the approach. At the point of flare-out a Flight Captain stationed in a mobile tower took over.

"Ease it back a little, Jayhawk. Not too fast. Wait till she's ready to stop flying. That's got it. Now hold her as she is—easy—easy. You're touching. Let her run a bit. Now easy on the brakes. That's it. More brakes. Take her down to ramp six and taxi back to your flight line."

It all went perfectly. And yet, when Kirk finally pulled back the canopy, he found himself shaking and bathed with sweat. He got out stiffly. Corliss had parked his plane and came to meet him.

"Not too tough, was it?" he grinned. "Well, you're a Sabre jockey—or part of one, anyhow. How's it feel?"

"Wonderful," said Kirk. "But I know I've still got a lot to learn."

Corliss chuckled. "Now that it's over for this morning," he said, "I'll tell you about another youngster I worked with last winter. Maybe you've heard the story. This lad had a good training record. He went through the instrument-check routine like a whiz. Then I got down off the cockpit ladder, and do you know what he did first thing? He reached out and retracted the landing gear! They say you could hear the crunch halfway to Vegas!"

Kirk roared with laughter. He didn't tell the lieutenant he had heard the yarn before, when he was here in Crew TAF. It was an old Nellis favorite, but funny just the same. Right now, after his first F-86 solo, he would have laughed at the oldest joke on record.

12

The three months' course moved fast. Flying the Sabrejet was hard work, even for old-timers. There was no loafing at the controls. You had to fly the fast jet every minute. Then, too, going on oxygen all the time at high altitudes was tiring. An hour of F-86 time was like two or three hours in a slower craft.

Kirk took half a dozen familiarization rides to get the complete feel of the airplane. Then, with Corliss still coaching him, he went up twice for all-out practice in acrobatics —the kind of top-speed maneuvering that might be called for in a dogfight. And each time he flew he gained confidence.

Finally all four planes in Trout Flight took the air at once and started flying in formation. Ron MacLean's progress had kept pace with Kirk's, and they flew close enough sometimes to grin at each other. The formations were pretty loose at first. At the speed they were moving a straggler could be a mile behind before the flight leader missed him.

For the first few times an instructor flew in No. 4 position

on the left rear wing, shepherding the formation and telling each man what he was doing wrong. Then, as they got the hang of it, the young pilots took turns at that post.

In squadron formation, the flights were renamed—Red, Green, Blue, and Yellow for standard identification. It was a proud day for Kirk when he pressed the radio button and called, "Red Leader to Tower. Red Flight approaching pattern from southeast at 1500 feet. Request landing clearance."

In their tenth week they started gunnery. The F-86 was armed with six .50-caliber guns and could carry eight rockets under each wing. For several days they practiced firing at fixed targets on the ground, diving and passing at high speed. And finally came air-to-air gunnery. Flying high in formation, they would peel off, one at a time, and head for a sack target towed behind a T-33.

Few of them hit it the first time around, for they found a

small, fast-moving object in the air was harder to get in the sights than a ground target. Kirk made the first clean hit on his third pass. After that the others began to get the hang of it.

The last phase of their training was the most exciting. Using gun cameras instead of ammunition, they went up to try their skill at what was called air tactics—the science of getting your gun-sights on an enemy plane without being shot down. There was a real element of danger in it that stirred Kirk's blood, for he knew what an air collision would do to planes flying close to the speed of sound.

They hunted in pairs during these mock hassles. When approaching planes were sighted, one pilot would go in to attack while the other flew cover for him to keep a possible opponent off his back and tail. "Hits" scored were surprisingly rare in these encounters. It took a keen eye to spot a plane three or four miles away, and when they were coming toward each other at a combined speed of 1200 miles an hour, the chance for a shot was gone in three seconds or less.

It was only when they climbed and twisted and succeeded in getting behind and above that they were able to hold an opponent in their sights long enough to register camera hits.

A hassle rarely lasted more than fifteen or twenty seconds. But in that time they covered miles of territory and climbed or dived thousands of feet. It was the most exacting flying Kirk had ever done—and the biggest thrill. He would land at the end of such a session bone-tired but always conscious that he was gaining in skill. Every day he learned new respect for the United Nations' pilots who were holding the MIG's in check over Korea.

He heard a good deal about MIG-15's in his ground-school classes. The instructors were men who had seen them in action and at close range, and they never belittled the abilities of the Russian-built fighters. MIG performance at high altitudes was actually better than that of the F-86C. Smaller and lighter, with a good jet engine, it could climb straight up and very fast. Its armament consisted of 20-millimeter and 37-millimeter cannons—considerably heavier than the Sabre's .50-caliber guns. There were photos of Red airplanes taken from different positions, too. One of the things Kirk learned was to identify the various types—especially the MIG-15—when a split second glimpse was thrown on the screen.

Then, as their training time at Nellis grew shorter, they were given the latest intelligence on Communist air tactics. In two years of fighting, the picture had changed several times. At the beginning, most of the MIG's sighted were close to the Yalu River line. They would go up in swarms

106

from their field at Antung but only rarely crossed over into territory where the UN held air superiority. It was a period of build-up and training for the Red pilots.

By May and June of 1951, the MIG's were growing bolder, flying as far south as Pyongyang and attacking formations of B-29's in spite of fighter escort. In a single big engagement on July 8, over a hundred MIG's tackled a strong group of Superforts. They succeeded in downing two, but supporting F-86 and F-84 fighters destroyed fourteen MIG's, probably destroyed ten more, and damaged twenty.

That summer the UN pilots found the enemy using a new kind of tactic. American airmen called it the "yo-yo." A large group of MIG's would circle over an F-86 formation at very high altitude. Part of them would come swooping down and fake an attack, then climb back upstairs while the UN jets chased them. Immediately the rest of the MIG's would drop down, trying to get on the Sabres' tails. The best way to beat the yo-yo attack was to spiral downward to altitudes where the MIG's lost the advantage they held higher up.

Through the fall of 1951 and during the first four months of 1952, enemy air activity was largely confined to intensive training over North Korea. There was a noticeable drop in the aggressiveness and skill of the Red pilots. Apparently most of the MIG's were being flown by learners, and they usually scuttled to safety as soon as Sabres came in sight. But in May, June, and July another change took place. Once again the Communists sent out their experienced fliers. There were more chances for real combat, even though the MIG's came south in smaller numbers.

These Red veterans were tough. They devised new tactics that were successful for a time. One of these used ground radar to send MIG formations into cloud cover above the path of UN bombers and fighters. They would appear so suddenly out of the overcast that occasionally they caught their intended victims by surprise.

Another trick they developed was the "end-run." A few MIG's would decoy the F-86's off in one direction while the main enemy group skirted around behind them to attack bombers or reconnaissance aircraft.

The lieutenant colonel who was doing the briefing stood at ease before them, hands in pockets, chewing a cold cigar. He was a blocky, square-jawed Pennsylvanian with a Polish name, who had been recalled from civilian life in 1950 and fought for two years in Korea. In 130 missions his record was five MIG's certainly destroyed and two probables.

"Every time they come up with a new tactic like that," he said, "we find an answer. It's the same as in football. Against a smart team a trick won't work but once. Those Commie pilots are getting better all the time but so are our boys. We're still clobbering 'em. The score still stands at eight to one—about 400 MIG's shot down to fifty or so of ours."

He paused to scratch a match and light his cigar while a hundred pilots in the big room waited, silent and intent.

"That sounds as if the odds are easy," he went on. "They aren't. You'll have a lot to learn over there before you're real tigers. You'll fly mission after mission and never see a MIG. Then when you do get one in your sights, he's likely to beat it back across the Yalu and thumb his nose at you. It's pretty frustrating—that Yalu line."

He grinned and drew in a puff of smoke. "We don't know," he said, "just how many of those MIG jockeys are Chinese. Most of 'em are. But one had to bail out a few months ago, and the Sabre pilot flew past close enough to get a good look at him. Our Intelligence boys won't commit themselves, but from all I've heard, guys with blue eyes an' blond hair are mighty rare in China."

*   *   *

They celebrated their final day at Nellis with a dress parade and a fly-over in formation. The whole Wing took part. As Red leader, Kirk spearheaded the big V of Jayhawk Squadron, flying in the No. 3 slot on the left flank of the Tigers.

Fifty miles out over the desert they gave their planes full throttle and started down from 40,000 feet. Three minutes later they were in level flight at 10,000, flying very close to the speed of sound. Not a Sabre was out of position as they screamed over the base.

Climbing for another few minutes, the formation executed a 180-degree turn and came over again, this time right "on the deck" at 300 feet and going full out. It must have been quite a spectacle from the ground. Kirk could see crew men ducking and putting their hands over their ears to shut out the deafening roar. Then in a flash the base was gone, and he was busy holding position as they climbed once more.

Every plane in the Wing got down without mishap, though it took time and some of the last to land were running low on fuel. The young pilots all thought it had been a good performance, and the Commanding Colonel agreed with them in a farewell speech that afternoon. After supper there was an impressive Retreat formation. Most of the men went into Las Vegas for a final fling, but after dinner in town with them Kirk came back to his quarters, wrote a letter or two, and did some packing.

He had a sober feeling about this last night on the base. The long build-up was over now—the years of training completed. When he first enlisted, he had dreamed about taking an active part in the Korean struggle, and it looked now as

109

if he would soon get his wish. He wondered about some of the others who had started with him at Lackland—Elmer Gamble and Tony Canuso, for instance. The Air Force was a big outfit, scattered all over the world, and he had no idea where they might be now. Ginnie Gordon, he did know, was in Japan. Earlier he had heard she was at a WAF Officer Candidate School. Perhaps by now she, too, would be wearing second lieutenant's bars.

In the morning he woke feeling fine, chuckling at the moans of the Las Vegas roisterers. Most of them, including Ron MacLean, were heavy-eyed and complained of headaches. However, they dressed on time and stood formation, for this was the day they would get their assignments as full-fledged Sabre pilots.

After morning chow they filed into the dayroom and were briefed. Then, as their names were called, each man stepped up to receive his packet of orders. Kirk caught up with Ron outside.

"What's yours say, Ron?" he asked.

"McChord AFB," MacLean replied with a grin. "How about you?"

"The same. That means Korea—or Japan anyhow. McChord's up near Tacoma, Washington. It's a MATS base for foreign clearance, and it's on the West Coast, so we're headed for Pacific duty. Come on—let's pack."

Forty or fifty other jet pilots were headed for the same destination. They took off that night in a C-54 transport that got them into McChord about dawn. To Kirk, used to the lightning speed of a Sabre, the moonlit landscape drifted by with painful slowness. He smiled when he thought of his first flight in an old C-47 and the thrill it had given him.

None of them had done much sleeping on the plane, but after checking in at the base, they were given the rest of the day off. Kirk and Ron put in a few hours of sack time, then went out about four o'clock to see what this Puget Sound country was like.

The September sunshine had broken through the clouds. Looking toward the east, Kirk suddenly grabbed his friend's arm.

"Gosh!" he whispered. "Do you suppose it's real or some kind of a mirage?"

He was pointing upward at a misty golden cone that seemed to rise halfway up the sky.

"It must be Mt. Rainier," Ron said. "I've heard about it, but I'd never have believed it stood up so high."

They took a bus into Tacoma and strolled along the water front, staring in wonder at the huge log booms and the sawmills with their towering sawdust burners. Then, after eating Dungeness crab in a good restaurant, they climbed a hillside street into a residential area. From the heights they could look north across the Sound to fir-clad islands and see the lights of tugs and freighters moving through the dusk. A strange, pleasant smell drifted up to them—a fragrance compounded of salt water and seaweed and fresh-cut lumber.

There had been nothing like this in Texas, Arizona, or Nevada. To Kirk, bred in the midlands, it was a stirring discovery. He turned to his companion.

"Ron," he asked, "have you ever seen the ocean?"

"Not exactly. But I took a lake boat all the way to Buffalo once. I guess Lake Erie's pretty much the same. Anyhow, if that MATS transport's ready for us tomorrow, we'll be seeing an awful lot of ocean and not much else for a day or two. By the way, hadn't we better think about getting back to the base? I'd like another good night's sleep in the U.S.A. before we take off, and those quarters at McChord are mighty comfortable."

They went down the hill and boarded the bus. Before he turned in, Kirk put in a long distance call to Clarksdale.

Central Daylight Saving Time made it three hours later there—a fact he had forgotten. His father's sleepy voice answered. For a moment he seemed to have trouble understanding that it was actually Kirk on the phone. Then he let out a shout that roused the rest of the household. They all talked breathlessly till the young pilot's three minutes were up, and he hunted through his pockets in vain for extra change.

"Well—good-by, Mom—good-by, Dad—and Margie," he told them. "I'll mail you a post card from wherever they're sending me!" And before they could ask any more questions, the connection was cut off.

The pilots were sleeping soundly in their luxurious beds in the McChord Bachelor Officers' Quarters when an orderly roused them at 0300.

"Sorry to wake you, sir," he told Kirk, "but your transport's fueling up right now. She'll be ready to take off in half an hour."

He went on to the next bed and the next while Kirk stumbled out and dressed. Fortunately his gear was still packed. He found Ron MacLean gulping coffee and doughnuts in the dayroom and joined him in a hasty breakfast. Then the group of pilots straggled out to the flight line lugging their B-4 bags.

It was chilly on the field and pitch dark except for the rows of hooded landing lights. A big double-decked C-97 loomed up in front of them. A captain checked their names on the list he held. "Next stop Hickam Field," he told them as they climbed aboard.

13

Hickam Field! Kirk had been only a little boy on the December Sunday in 1941 when that name was suddenly blasted into the news. But he had never forgotten. Pearl Harbor and Hickam Field, where the Navy and the Army Air Corps had been caught unprepared.

It was eight or nine hours' flying time to Hawaii in the big Boeing transports. They should be there by noon, he thought, as he settled himself comfortably. Meanwhile, there was nothing to see so he might as well sleep.

The glint of sunlight on the sea woke him at 0900. The immense emptiness of the Pacific, stretching away to the curved horizon, fascinated him. Twelve thousand feet below he saw a speck that must be a freighter. Otherwise there was nothing but the unbelievable expanse of water.

They got coffee and sandwiches and set their watches two hours back to Honolulu time. Some of the men napped again; others read or played gin rummy, while the big engines droned on. At last there was a call over the loudspeaker from the cockpit.

"Islands in sight. We'll be letting down over Diamond Head in five minutes."

There was a rush to the windows. Along the line of sky and sea Kirk made out two dark patches—Molokai off to the left and Oahu directly ahead. The rhythm of the engines changed. The rocky shape of the famous promontory drew nearer and with it the darker mountains beyond. Then they could see white surf on a short, curved beach, the buildings of a city, and the wide basin of Pearl Harbor.

The C-97 touched down at 1130 and the men got out,

113

looking around them at the fringing palms and structures of Hickam Field. There was an excellent lunch waiting for them. After that, while the big plane was being checked and refueled, they had time to buy a trinket or two and breathe the soft, flower-scented trade wind. Kirk could see why older, more settled Air Force men liked to be stationed in Hawaii.

They were in the air once more by 1500, winging westward. Kirk was sound asleep in his seat when, a little after midnight, the pilot announced it wasn't Monday evening any more. It was Wednesday morning. They had crossed the international date line and Tuesday was gone—just where, nobody seemed to know.

About 0100 the plane let down again, this time aiming for a tiny dot that lay alone in the immense expanse of the Pacific. There was no South Seas glamor on Wake Island. All they found when they got out was coral sand and gony birds and corrugated metal Quonset huts. They ate a tasteless concoction of powdered eggs, drank some coffee, and stretched their legs while more gas was pumped into the wing tanks. Finally, at 0300 of a black night, they clambered aboard the transport again.

Now they were on the last long over-water lap, the run northwestward to Japan. At sun-up Kirk was wide awake. Most of the others rose and stretched, too conscious of the approaching end of their journey to do any more dozing. Normal flying time from Wake to Haneda Airport was eight hours, but as they passed through two more time zones, it was only 0900 that morning, Tokyo time, when they sighted the white cone of Fuji, a hundred miles away on their left.

Haneda looked like any big city airport at home. The main difference was in the grinning little brown ground crew men who bustled everywhere. The pilots and their luggage were loaded on rickety buses and trundled up the road to an Air Force installation at Fuchu. There the inevitable processing began. It lasted all that day with time out for a couple of hasty meals.

Kirk was fagged out by the time it was over. He had slept only in cat naps for three days, and his eating had been sketchy and irregular. At last, well along in the evening, Air Force buses took the new arrivals to Tachikawa AB, a troop carrier base that lay some twenty miles west of Tokyo. There they fell into bed and enjoyed the luxury of eight solid hours of sleep.

A colonel briefed them after morning chow, giving them an outline of their training during the next few months. It seemed they would not do any real combat flying before the end of the year. First they had to spend three or four weeks at Johnson AFB, going through a special ground school. Then, if they were lucky, they would move on to one of the F-86 bases in Korea, where they would be taken into experienced squadrons as replacements for pilots who had been lost, wounded, or rotated home. In the meantime, the colonel warned them to be on their good behavior. The Japanese were a proud, touchy people, and it was important to international relations that they should think well of American soldiers, sailors, and airmen.

Johnson Air Force Base was near a little town called Irumagawa, only a dozen miles away. They got there late in the afternoon, riding across country in jeeps from the Tachikawa motor pool. It was an introduction to the real Japan.

"Hey, look at that, Kayo!" Ron exclaimed as they passed a row of tiny vegetable plots. "Barefooted farmers in those wide hats!"

"I know," Kirk grinned. "It's like a TV travelogue. And there's a Mama-San with a baby on her back. These people deserve to get ahead. All of 'em sure work like beavers."

Johnson wasn't one of the biggest U.S. bases in Japan, but the boys had heard about it back in the states—its good quarters and fabulous Officers' Club. They were assigned rooms in the B.O.Q. and unpacked their gear. That evening Kirk and Ron went into the city to see the sights.

"You any idea how big Tokyo is?" Kirk asked as they got off the bus.

"Pretty big," his friend answered. "I'd guess as big as Chicago—maybe four million?"

Kirk had looked it up. "You're way short," he said. "Close to seven million. That's almost up to New York and London."

It wasn't as impressive as they had hoped, though some of the new office buildings, erected since the war, were handsome enough. What they missed was the flavor of the Orient. Nearly everyone on the streets in midtown was dressed in the American and European fashion.

They found a restaurant with a juke-box, where a lot of
Army and Air Force men were eating, and ordered suki-
yaki for supper. It turned out to be a kind of stew, tasty
enough. Ron tried a cup of rice wine. He smacked his lips
over it, but Kirk noticed he didn't finish his drink.

That was the extent of their big night in Tokyo. Next
morning, back at the base, they were put to work in earnest.
There was a great deal of knowledge they must absorb in
three tough weeks of ground school. And practically all of
it came under the heading of Escape and Evasion.

The man who talked to them the first day made an impression on Kirk that he would never forget. He was a tall,
lean captain with a triple row of ribbons above his pilot's
wings. His face was lined, and he walked with a cane.

"One of the big differences between our Air Force and
the Reds'," he said abruptly, "is that they consider their

pilots expendable. We don't. If anything happens to your planes, we want to get you back in one piece and breathing. That's why you're being given this course. That's why you're issued a survival kit. That's why we've got helicopters and brave men flying 'em.

"Just so you'll understand, I'm going to tell you my own story. It started one afternoon in April, 1951, when my B-26 got an engine afire north of the enemy lines. Feathering the prop didn't do any good. I told the gunner and navigator to bail out, and I followed.

"I picked a poor spot—a steep hillside full of rocks—and landed pretty hard. Both bones of my left leg were broken below the knee. I got out of my chute and crawled downhill, hoping to hide in a ditch. Then I heard voices coming over the hill—enemy voices. I took out my .45 and waited.

"It wasn't easy, for my leg was hurting like the devil. I opened my first-aid kit and managed to give myself a shot of morphine. Meanwhile, the enemy soldiers I'd heard were hunting for me, but they kept under cover because our aircraft were overhead.

"I tried to signal the planes with my signal mirror but didn't know whether they'd caught it. After about forty-five minutes a North Korean soldier suddenly came up from behind me and yelled 'Surrender!' in English. He had me covered with his machine gun, so I said 'Yes.' He took my .45 pistol, saw my leg was broken, and began searching my pockets.

"About then two more North Koreans arrived—an officer and a young enlisted man in his 'teens. They all had Russian PPHS machine guns. They took my camera, wrist watch, pistol and shoulder holster, a can of C-rations, Mae West, escape kit, plastic water bag, two first-aid kits and a shaving kit. Then they motioned me to follow them. I did my best to crawl after them, but the officer came back and hit me in the thigh with his machine gun butt, trying to make me hurry.

"The aircraft had them nervous, so two of them went up the hill while the first soldier stayed with me. They yelled back at him—apparently told him to kill me. He looked startled, but he aimed the machine gun at my head, mumbling something that sounded like an apology.

" 'No,' I told him quietly, 'you don't want to do that.' He was standing very close to me, and I could see him hesitate. Then I grabbed the gun barrel and jerked him right into my lap. He did hold onto the gun, though. Must have fired twenty rounds that went wild and hit the ground beside me. When he screamed, the other two came running back. They were about ten feet away when I turned the gun muzzle on them. The soldier was still holding onto it, but I pulled the trigger. Nothing happened. The bolt was jammed.

"The kid tried to shoot at me, but I was a lot bigger than the one I was wrestling with, and I swung him around as a shield. When the youngster came closer to get a clear shot, I kicked him in the chin with my good foot. He fell on top of me, and I grabbed him with one arm, held on to the other soldier, and managed to bang their heads together till they were groggy. They struggled up and pulled me up with them, just as the officer came rushing down holding my .45.

"For a minute or so I was able to keep the two soldiers between me and the pistol. Finally the officer fired at my head. I felt the bullet crease my scalp as I ducked. I knew my number was up if I didn't do something, so I moaned and spun to the ground, as if he'd killed me. Just then he fired a second shot that went through my flying suit and took a nick out of my right shoulder. I lay face down on the ground playing dead.

"By this time the planes in our air cover had seen the

scrap and were making low passes. That scared the Red soldiers, and they left in a hurry. After I was sure they were gone, I crawled down the hill to a drainage ditch. There was a lot of firing at the aircraft from the hill, and I knew the copter couldn't land there, so I hoisted myself over the dyke into a rice paddy.

"I rested awhile and pushed my way on my back out into the middle of the paddy. One of our planes spotted me, and I pointed at the hill with my arm. The B-26's and F-80's went at it then, and a real war broke out, with incessant firing on both sides. Five minutes later the copter came in, right through the flying bullets. It settled down about ten feet away, and a couple of medical corpsmen got me aboard before any of us were hit. Next thing I knew they had me in a forward area hospital.

"I was lucky, I guess, for they picked me up when I'd been on the ground only an hour and a half. There have been others—hurt worse than I was—who spent weeks hiding and crawling and starving and freezing before they made it back to our lines. You'll hear from some of them in the next three weeks, and if you want to stay alive, you'll remember every word they say."

He nodded, stiff and unsmiling, and limped back to his chair. The young pilots had been sitting in utter silence. Now they stirred again and rustled their notebooks. He had brought the fighting close to them.

They had been given lectures on survival before, but from that moment on they paid closer attention. Every one of them realized that this was the real thing.

They practiced bandaging themselves and learned how to use the material in the first-aid kit. Other lessons covered how to keep from freezing in the bitter Korean winter weather and how to build a lean-to shelter out of a parachute. They studied all kinds of native roots and berries,

finding out which ones were nourishing and which might
cause sickness. They even experimented with eating raw rice
and raw fish and were warned that some fish were poisonous.

It was amazing how much useful equipment was contained in the survival kit. Before they got through, they gave
careful study to every item in it—such as the knife, the compass, the flares, the signaling mirror, the fishhooks, the tablets for purifying water, and the "blood chit," printed on
cloth in Korean, which would explain their mission, give
their blood type, and promise a reward for their safe return
if they should be lucky enough to fall among friendly
people.

For nearly a month they lived, ate, and slept with the
subject of survival. And every man among them must have
wondered, as Kirk did, if he would ever have to test his
knowledge in the rugged hills beyond the enemy line.

14

Kirk and Ron were too much occupied with their work to go
anywhere off post during that intensive training period. But
at the end of the course, early in November, everybody felt
ready to blow off some steam. There was a celebration at
the Officers' Club that night. The two young pilots put on
their freshly pressed dress blues, polished their buttons and
bars, and followed the crowd to the clubhouse.

At their table was a combat flying instructor—a cigar-
chewing F-86 veteran named Maguire, who had been in
Japan and Korea for years.

"Anything you boys want to know," he told them expan-
sively, "ol' Mike Maguire can tell you. Like, for instance"
—he pointed his cigar at a grinning Japanese waiter a few

tables away—"that guy's got quite a story. Johnson used to be at a Jap Kamikaze base back in the big war. An' Toji, there, was a Kamikaze pilot. He'd finished his training an' was just about to take off for his suicide bomb dive on a Yankee warship when V-J Day came. So he just hung around here until the Air Force took over the base, an' now he's a bartender at the NCO Club. I guess they borrowed him to-night for the big doings here. You ought to try one o' his Kamikaze cocktails. I don't know what's in them, but they're bombs, all right."

Smiling, the boys declined. They had heard the legend before. Probably every Jap civilian on the base had been described at one time or another as the famous Toji.

It was a big, gay crowd, and when the dancing started, the floor was jammed. There seemed to be plenty of girls—WAF officers and Air Force nurses in uniform, besides a contingent of post wives and daughters. Kirk was in the stag line looking for a partner, when a couple danced past him. And suddenly, over a captain's shoulder, he was staring into a pair of cornflower-blue eyes. For a moment he stood there gaping. Then the girl looked back, and he knew it was Ginnie.

He never stopped to wonder about the etiquette of cutting in on a senior officer. He darted after them and tapped the man on the arm. "Pardon me, sir," he blurted, "but—may I? Miss Gordon's a—well—"

Ginnie was blushing. "It's all right, Captain," she laughed. "Meet Lieutenant Owen—Captain Simms. You see, Kirk's an old friend. I'm sure you won't mind."

A moment later he was holding her close, circling slowly among the packed couples.

"You're really here!" she murmured. "Oh, Kirk, I'm so glad! And I never dreamed you'd be sent to Johnson. I've

122

only been here a month myself, so you wouldn't have had a letter."

She pulled away a little so that she could admire his wings and bars.

"They're mighty becoming," she said. "I knew you'd make it. And how do you like mine?"

"Perfect!" he told her with a grin. "You'd better stay a second lieutenant, though, because the gold matches your hair."

The music ended, and he took her back to his table to meet Ron. The young Detroiter was openly admiring. He had been stuck for the last dance with the buxom daughter of a colonel, and his first question was whether Ginnie had a friend. It took her only a moment to produce one, almost as attractive as herself, and from then on the evening was a tremendous success.

When it was over, they walked the girls home through the sharp November night.

"How long will you be here, Kirk?" Ginnie asked. "Long enough to see me again?"

"I sure hope so. We've got a week of concentrated flying coming up—combat stuff. Then we'll move along to Korea. Don't know where yet. Probably a rear area where we'll be put in combat squadrons. Anyhow, we know we'll have a week."

She pressed his arm gently, and they were silent for a few steps.

"Will you—will you think about marrying me, Ginnie?" he gulped. "When it's over and we can go home?"

"Then," she whispered, "or tomorrow—or when you like. The answer is yes."

*　　*　　*

That week the young pilots flew three and four times a day. They took the jets up in all kinds of weather, flying in team formation with men who had completed their missions in Korea and knew all the tricks of MIG combat. It was tough, tense work, every minute of it, and the boys began to realize how little they really knew.

Kirk had started the week in a sort of rosy cloud. The concentration of flying sobered him in a hurry, but he still had time to see Ginnie twice before his time at Johnson AFB was ended. They didn't talk much. She had seen enough of this strange half-war to know that not all jet pilots came back. She was content to be with him, and Kirk felt the same way. It was hardly fair to make any plans.

On the final Saturday he took all his savings, went into Tokyo, and bought a small diamond ring at a reputable jeweler's. She had it on her hand when they said good-by that night, and she smiled through tears that were as bright as the little stone itself.

Kirk and Ron got their orders next morning. They were assigned as replacements in a famous Fighter-Interceptor Wing at Kimpo and were told to report at a C-54 transport plane of the 315th Troop Carrier Command that afternoon. At 1400 they were aboard with their duffel. The transport flew westward, skirting the great white cone of Fuji, then crossed a ten-thousand-foot range beyond and roared out over the gray waters of the Sea of Japan.

By that time the older pilots, returning after leave, had given the youngsters a better idea of where they were bound. It was the great fighter base at Kimpo, near Seoul. Every man who could get a view out a window was watching with tense interest when the Korean coast came in sight. There was a seaport city down there at the left, with a good many ships in the harbor. That, they knew, must be Pusan, the last foothold of the South Korean and UN troops when they were nearly pushed into the sea two years before. Then they were flying northwestward over a rugged brown landscape dotted with farms and miserable villages.

They could see trains crawling north toward the front and long strings of military trucks on the roads. Those communication lines would have made fine targets for bombing and strafing by enemy planes, Kirk thought. But he knew they were safe. The F-86 squadrons had kept the upper hand in the air for many months now, regardless of the odds they faced. His spine tingled at the realization that soon he would be joining that gallant crew.

It was dark when they landed, and they stumbled, cold and hungry, across the field to the lighted brick building that housed the Wing Headquarters where they were to report. The staff sergeant who checked their orders was someone Kirk was sure he had seen before—a big, sandy-haired man with a square Irish jaw. He hesitated over Kirk's papers and took a second look. Then he stood up, smiling.

"Lieutenant Owen," he said, "I guess you wouldn't remember me. The name's Brodie, sir. I was the recruiter who swore you in back in Clarksdale. Welcome to Kimpo."

Kirk grinned and shook his hand. "It's good to see somebody from home, Sergeant," he told him. "I knew your face was familiar. How long have you been here?"

"A little over a year. Soon as I've checked the rest o' these orders, I'll run you over to your quarters."

He drove Kirk and Ron a mile or more in his jeep to a low, barnlike barracks building. Each man had a sagging cot, a chair, and a locker. It was cold, and the only heat came from a sheet-iron stove. They were tired enough to turn in as soon as they had unpacked.

After a night's sleep and a good breakfast the new men of the squadron assembled in the briefing room. There a quiet-spoken major sat on the corner of a table and started talking to them.

"This is a Fighter-Interceptor Wing," he said. "You can all fly F-86 fighter planes or you wouldn't be here. But you won't be doing any fighting—not yet. The F-86E is an excellent airplane. You might say it's a good tool in the hands of a skilled workman. But it isn't F-86's that keep us on top. It's the guts and courage and know-how of the men who fly them."

The major eased himself off the desk and stood erect, his eyes snapping. "Only one kind of men belong in this outfit," he said. "Tigers! I know you've heard the word before. Maybe you think it just means hot pilots. I want to tell you a tiger is a good deal more than that. Besides fast reflexes and steady nerves and keen eyes, you've got to have the killer instinct. You've got to hate those Reds for what they are and for what they're trying to do to you, your family, your country, and everything you believe in. You've got to accept the fact that it's kill or be killed—get that MIG first or he'll get you.

"You are now joining the Tiger Squadron. It's named that for a reason. Any man here who has doubts about being a tiger had better say so at the start, for this is no place for him."

He paused to let the words sink in, and his eyes searched the face of every man in the room. Nobody smiled or moved.

"All right," he said. "For several weeks the squadron will be flying every day. Each of you will be assigned to a flight and to a two-plane element. Your wingmen will be veterans—old tigers who've done a lot of missions and know all the tricks. They'll ride herd on you during this shakedown period. And they'll still be with you when you're ready for combat—those of you who make it. Check out

126

your gear at Operations and report on the flight line at 0900.”

The impact of the major’s words had gone deep. There was no skylarking and little talk among the new pilots as they made their way to Flight Operations. They were soberly taking stock of themselves.

The word “killer” was still ringing in Kirk’s ears. It was an ugly word—one he had never thought of applying to himself. Perhaps he wasn’t a real tiger after all. A good upbringing—church and Sunday School and faith in God— did they fit a man for this job?

He was still torn by doubts when he climbed into the shiny new F-86E. A captain named French—a lean, relaxed young man who looked only a few years older than Kirk— stood on the ladder beside him while he went through the cockpit check. He must have noticed Kirk’s preoccupation.

“Something on your mind?” he asked. “Maybe Major Groome’s ‘tiger’ talk? Snap out of it, Owen! I can tell you it’s not that bad—and right now you’ve got a Sabre to fly. Okay?”

His grin was reassuring. Kirk saw him go back to the next plane and get in, waving a hand in encouragement. Five minutes later they were in the air. The thrill of the surging climb swept the trouble out of Kirk’s mind for the time at least, and he devoted all his energy to showing the wingman that he could fly.

They cruised and stunted for the better part of an hour, mostly at high altitude. Captain French kept Kirk’s headphones hot with a running fire of comment on the countryside spread beneath them.

“That’s Seoul over yonder on the left,” he would say. “And there’s the fighter-bomber base at Suwon. Looks like a bunch of F-80’s loading up to hit the supply routes north of Pyongyang. Way over to the right you can see Chunchon.

This whole country's been fought over three or four times—
nearly every mile of it. You wonder how these poor Korean
folks have the guts to hang on. Now we'll swing over west
and fly along the coast so you can have a look at the Yellow
Sea."

Kirk memorized the landmarks they crossed. The time
might come when he would need to know them.

"How far is the Yalu from here?" he asked over the
radio.

He heard French laugh. "Everybody wants to know that.
You won't get within 150 miles of the Yalu till you've had
more seasoning—maybe in a month."

They joined up with the other two planes in Blue Flight
and flew formation for a while. Ron MacLean was in the
No. 3 spot, close behind Kirk on the left.

"Well, Frenchie," a new voice drawled over the phone,
"think these kids'll ever make it? Mine don't look much
like a tiger, but durned if he don't smell like one!"

Ronnie chuckled. "Lieutenant Yokum," he said, "you
can insult me all you like, but be careful what you say
about my pal up front. Kayo, get acquainted with Li'l Abner
Yokum, from Arkansas—my new nursemaid."

After they landed, Kirk shook hands with First Lieutenant Yokum. From the Ozark twang of the voice he had
expected to see a long, gangling hill-billy type, but to his
surprise the man was short and stocky, with a round, pleasant face. The four had lunch together.

K-14 had been a disappointment to Kirk when he first
saw it in daylight. After the splendor of Johnson AFB it
looked shabby and makeshift. Some of the buildings had
been repaired but needed paint. The Officers' Club was old,
cluttered, and noisy. The hangars were well equipped, and
the pilots' quarters were clean, but everything looked bare
and worn. Even the runways had been patched.

When the older pilots mentioned some of the reasons during lunch, he was glad he hadn't been critical. Kimpo was one of the few UN bases the Reds had bombed. They had succeeded in getting through with a few night fighters and dropped their explosives before the avenging interceptors caught up with them.

"Any chance they'll be back?" Ron asked.

Captain French shrugged. "Might," he said, "but I doubt it. Ask our fat friend here. He was in on the scrap. What do you say, Yokum?"

"No," replied the Arkansan. "Don't believe they'll try it. Only one of 'em ever got home, an' the seat of his pants was smokin'. They gave me credit for two of 'em, but I reckon one didn't really count. There was three-four of us shootin' at him."

"You see," French put in quietly, "those bombs got some of our boys on the ground. One was a chap who'd gone through Basic with Yokum—best man at his wedding."

It took Kirk longer than usual to get to sleep that night. He thought about the major's briefing and about the Ten Commandments. "Thou shalt not kill." There was no quibbling in those words—no ifs, ands, or buts. Yet there was the story of David, certainly a nice, decent kid, brought up by those same rules. And David had stood up to Goliath—slain him with a rock out of the brook. Why? To protect his people. If he had run away, Goliath and the rest of the Philistines would have made the Israelites their slaves. Maybe, Kirk thought, that was the answer. When your freedom and the people you love are threatened, you've got to fight.

In the darkness he said a short, silent prayer, asking for guidance. Then, feeling better, he went to sleep.

15

The daily flying continued, and as the weeks passed, Kirk's respect for Captain Evan French, the "old tiger" who flew with him, steadily increased. French had won his wings as a nineteen-year-old in the summer of 1945. When the war ended, he stayed in another year, flying P-51's. Then he went home to Seattle, got married, and worked hard at his job with a big lumber firm. In 1950 he was called back to fight in Korea, leaving his wife and baby and the new suburban home he had built on Mercer Island.

He had eighty combat missions and two MIG's to his credit. Now he was sweating out the slow days until he got his well-deserved release from active duty. Kirk never heard him complain. He was quiet, understanding, and modest about his achievements, yet he had earned a reputation as a terrific fighter pilot. If this man was a tiger, Kirk thought, it would be an honor to be called one.

They covered a lot of Korea in those weeks. Kirk saw the country change from brown to white after a heavy snowfall in late November. His sympathy went out to the Infantry soldiers, huddled down there in their foxholes, and the drivers of supply and ammunition trucks who had to battle their way over icy roads.

Blue Flight cruised eastward to Samchok and Yangyang on the seacoast and all the way up to Wonsan, where gray UN warships cruised offshore. Then they crossed southwestward, following the Imjin River past Kaesong. On one such trip they flew a hundred miles up the coast of the Yellow Sea, dropping low enough to study the islands that lay offshore. Many of them had been taken by the Navy and cleared of Communists. These were known as "safe" islands —possible rescue points for pilots in trouble and unable to fly back to their bases. On a few of them there were even short landing strips, and most had caches of food and water.

On their return from these exploring flights, Kirk and Ron pored over their maps, checking the positions of the islands and landmarks they had seen. They were beginning to know Korea like their own back yards.

Tiger Squadron was only one of four in the Wing based at K-14. The other F-86 squadrons were all manned by combat-ready pilots and flew daily missions northward over the enemy lines to the strip along the Yalu known as MIG Alley. There were B-26's on the field as well, and their duty was to harass Red troop concentrations with small bombs, napalm, and machine-gun fire.

The briefing room was always filled with fighter pilots wearing their flying gear, waiting for the call to "scramble." Kirk and Ron spent a good deal of time there. They absorbed some added knowledge by listening to the talk—most of it in a kidding vein but occasionally serious.

Sometimes pilots didn't return from their missions. A flight would land, and there would be only three planes.

"Flak bad today?" someone would ask, and there would be a gruff answer.

"Yeah. Afraid Joe got it. He was afire at 2,000. I didn't see his parachute."

All the veterans had more respect for the Chinese anti-aircraft guns than for MIG-15 pilots. "When you're in a hassle with a MIG," one of them explained, "you can depend on your own flying and shooting to get you out. Flak can hit you all of a sudden, coming out of nowhere, and there isn't much you can do about it."

It didn't always end in tragedy when an airplane was ‹ shot down. Twice, during Kirk's probationary period, he heard of helicopter rescues. If a pilot's friends saw him bail out, there was always a good chance that they could call a "chopper" in to pick him up.

Among the stories the boys heard more than once was the account of the biggest single air strike in the Korean war—the destruction of the four huge hydroelectric plants six months before. Lieutenant Yokum had been in the middle of it.

"We got our briefin' the mornin' of 23 June," he told them. "It was a big one all right. More'n 500 planes—Air Force, Navy, an' Marines—everything from carrier fighters to Superforts. Our squadron was scheduled to fly cover for the bombers at Suiho, the big dam on the Yalu. There was a MIG base right across the river, an' we figured we'd get a real scrap when the bombs started fallin'.

"It all went off like clockwork. Right at the same minute, the attack hit four different targets much as 150 miles apart. Over to the east there was Fusen, Choshin, an' Kyosen. An' toppin' 'em all was Suiho. We came roarin' out of a heavy overcast at 1601 that afternoon. There were our big boys below us, an' right ahead was Suiho dam an' the reservoir backed up behind it.

"Those bombardiers didn't bother with the dam. They were plasterin' the generator plant on every pass. An' what were we doin' while it happened? Sittin' up there with our tongues hangin' out, watchin' four or five hundred MIG's over at the Antung base. They were all lined up, neat as you please, an' when the fireworks started, durned if they didn't take off an' head north! Not one of 'em tried to stop our bombers. They just beat it back into Manchuria. Heck—I'd reckoned on gettin' at least one that day, but no soap."

"Why didn't they come over and fight?" Ron asked. "Knocking out all their electric power must have made 'em mad enough."

"All we could figure," Yokum replied, "was they'd never seen that many planes before an' decided we were comin' to clobber their field. Golly—how I wish we could!" he sighed.

In that last wistful phrase was all the frustration felt by a thousand American pilots. It was the ground rules that made this a tough war.

*　　　*　　　*

Christmas was drawing near—Kirk's third Christmas in the Air Force. There wasn't much he could do about gifts, for the shops in Seoul were pitifully short of wares. By luck he found a small jade figurine for Ginnie and mailed it with his love. To his mother he sent a money order and asked her to buy presents with it.

On the nineteenth of December the thick weather that had covered central Korea for three days broke at last. Bright sun shone on the snow and the cleared runways.

"Got a surprise for you today," Captain French told Kirk with a grin. "Blue Flight's been promoted. We're heading north for a look-see. Better check the ammo belts on those guns."

Kirk's heart jumped. At long last he was going to get a glimpse of MIG Alley!

They took off with full loads of fuel at 1030 hours. The flight climbed to 30,000 feet, tested the guns by firing short bursts, and cruised northward at a fuel-saving 60 per cent of power.

Under them, clearly visible, the landscape unrolled. Munsan came in view, then Chandang and Kaesong. Kirk pressed the radio button.

"Blue leader to Flight Commander," he said. "Front lines must be close now, aren't they?"

"We'll be over them in a minute," French answered. "See the smoke down there? That's artillery fire."

The faint thudding sound came up to them after they passed overhead. Kirk saw the glint of metal on a tiny T-6 spotter plane moving slowly and very close to the hilly ground. Little black puffs of smoke surrounded the spotter, but he flew on, twisting and zigzagging, pinpointing targets for the UN guns. It made Kirk shiver. That kind of flying took real skill and daring.

On they went, past the big town of Pyongyang. "All right, boys," came French's voice over the radio. "Keep your eyes peeled in all directions. From now on we could see hostiles any time."

They cruised steadily north, maintaining altitude. Sinanju and Anju passed beneath them, and they saw a bay cutting deep into the land. They overtook a flight of B-29's and got a glimpse of the bomb bursts as the big planes worked over a railroad bridge.

Far ahead and a little above them Kirk thought he detected specks in the sky.

"Planes," he called quickly. "One o'clock high."

"Roger, Blue leader," said French. "Let's go upstairs and take a look. Full power."

Ten seconds later they could see the dots clearly. There were four of them—F-86E's—cruising on a course parallel to their own. French talked to them and found they were a flight from Suwon.

"Been here twenty minutes," they said. "No MIG's. Guess we'll let you take over."

When the Suwon quartet had departed southward, Blue Flight swung west at reduced speed. They were in MIG Alley now, with the Yalu in sight away to their right.

"See that big lake?" French asked. "That's the Suiho reservoir. Antung and the MIG bases are just a few miles beyond, so keep on the ball."

They patrolled the area for a quarter of an hour or more, constantly watching above, below, and all around them. Twice they encountered other F-86 flights which had no more to report than they did. Finally, when their fuel was half gone and they were beginning to think of going back, Tiger Red Flight from K-14 came into view.

"Anything doing?" the new arrivals asked eagerly. "Shot down any MIG's yet?"

"Not a MIG," Kirk replied. "Haven't even seen one. Hope you have better luck."

Blue Flight was about to start for home when French's voice came over the radio. "You've heard all about flak," he said. "Maybe you ought to know what it looks and sounds like. Push up your throttles and power dive to 20,000. Let's see what happens."

When Kirk pulled out of the dive, he was going better than 700 miles an hour, still on full throttle. Suddenly a white puff bloomed below him, and there was a thudding explosion. Others followed quickly. As he pulled up into a climb, he heard the sharp rattle of metal against his fuselage. Only when he had gained another five thousand feet, did he look around for the rest of the flight. French was still there on his wing. The others were far ahead, flying level at 20,000. Apparently no damage had been done.

"Sorry," the captain told him. "That was a little closer than I expected. Still, you know now how it feels to be shot at, and you won't underestimate those Commie gunners."

Back at the base they landed with fuel to spare. Kirk climbed out and took a look at the underbody of the plane. There it was—a good-sized dent and a three-cornered tear in the aluminum alloy skin. A shell fragment had done it, but luckily there was no serious damage. He showed it to the crew chief and was told it could be repaired in a matter of hours.

They flew every day between then and Christmas. There was a strange quiet on the Chinese side of the Yalu, and only a few contacts with MIG fighters were reported. Veteran pilots who had three or four kills to their credit and were sweating out their ace rating made no secret of their disgruntlement.

Captain Evan French laughed at their remarks. "All I want," he said, "is to get in the rest of my missions and head for Seattle. I've got a kid back home, and I reckon he and Mary need me more than the Air Force does."

On Christmas Eve, Kirk received letters and gifts from Clarksdale and Johnson Air Force Base. Ginnie sent him a silver identification bracelet with his name and serial number. The presents from home were practical but welcome. His mother had made him a pair of warm, hand-knit wool socks, which fitted nicely inside his winter flying boots. That night he went to a midnight service at the base chapel.

With the loved, familiar strains of Christmas carols still ringing in his ears, he went to sleep.

The major sent his orderly to the barracks with a message on Christmas morning.

"You'll all be in the briefing room in half an hour," he told them abruptly. "Major Groome says the enemy may have the mistaken impression that Christians don't work on 25 December. We want to be prepared for 'em."

The squadron was prompt. Every man showed up five minutes early with full flying gear. The morning hours dragged by, and nothing happened. Some of the boys played bridge or read magazines. Others dozed. At noon sandwiches and coffee were brought in to them.

Suddenly, at 1245, there was a buzzing on the loudspeaker, and a voice brought them all to attention.

"This is Wing Command," the voice barked. "Large numbers of enemy aircraft are reported taking off at Antung. This is a general alert—repeat—general alert to all fighter squadrons. Pilots, man your planes."

They went out on the run, adjusting their helmets while

they scrambled. Blue Flight was in the air within five minutes, falling into position behind the four F-86's of Red Flight as soon as they had altitude. Over on the right the Greens were climbing, too. Tiger Squadron leveled out in loose formation at 30,000 feet and cut power to cruising speed. There was a heavy cloud cover over the landscape, but they were far above it, flying in brilliant sunshine.

A little after 1300 they began picking up scraps of talk over the radio—short, disconnected phrases like "Going up, Charlie—get on his tail!" . . . "Four o'clock low—six bogies!"

Eagerly Kirk scanned the sky ahead. Somebody had found MIG's, and he hoped they'd still be there when the Tigers got on the scene. Then he saw faint contrails of white against the blue.

"Squadron Commander to Tiger Flights," the major called. "Break away by elements. Drop your tanks and get ready for action. Over."

Kirk got rid of the wing tanks and peeled off with French close behind him. They cut to the right, away from the others. The contrails were still in sight, and now the boy could see the darting specks that made them. He pushed up the throttle and climbed to get above the hassle.

"Two of ours," said French laconically. "They've got some bandits on the run. Don't believe they need us. Let's find some of our own."

Within seconds Kirk got his first real view of a MIG-15. One of the enemy planes in the dogfight had climbed to take evasive action. He was directly in front of them now and coming their way.

"Twelve o'clock even!" Kirk yelled and tried to line the MIG up with the "pipper" on his sight. Before he could fire, the Russian-built fighter whizzed past. Kirk jerked the F-86 into a tight wing-over and gunned after the vanishing dot.

It was no use. The MIG pilot had evidently had all he wanted. Kirk saw him bank toward the Yalu and dive for the cloud cover two miles below.

"Let him go," said French. "You'd just risk a collision down in that soup."

They cruised for several minutes without sighting any more of the enemy. Then the major came on the radio ordering the Tigers home. "We'll rendezvous over Sonchon at angels thirty," he said, meaning an altitude of 30,000 feet.

Sonchon was only a short distance to the south, and enough glimpses of the ground were visible through the overcast to give them their bearings. Within five minutes the last element had joined the formation, and they were heading for their base.

The radio buzzed with conversation as the pilots compared notes. Yokum, it appeared, was the only one who had scored a sure hit. His quarry had been definitely afire when it dove into the cloud bank, and he would be credited with a probable.

They climbed out of their planes in a jubilant mood, ready for the turkey dinner. That was Christmas at K-14.

16

Kirk wrote to Ginnie two or three times a week, answering her letters and telling as much as security regulations allowed about his own activities. Blue Flight was cruising north every day now. For a while Captain French tried to keep them out of combat, but Kirk and Ron were itching for action. By mid-January, they had seen distant enemy formations a number of times and had really been close on one or two occasions.

Meanwhile, they still had some ground-school work to cover. They were lectured on combat tactics and on escape and evasion techniques. Their gear was inspected regularly, and they were quizzed on the use of the equipment they carried.

There was a good deal of it. Sometimes Kirk wondered if it was all necessary. When he got into his F-86E for a mission to MIG Alley, he wore a G-suit, Mae West, heavy, fleece-lined flying boots, flight jacket, folded dinghy and parachute. In the pockets and otherwise distributed about his person were his .45-caliber pistol in its shoulder holster, a can of C-rations, a plastic water bag, first-aid kit, shaving kit, prayer book, wrist watch, a flashlight, a big jackknife, and the E & E kit that contained a small magnetic compass, flares, a signaling mirror, fishhooks and line, matches in a waterproof container, water-purifying tablets, a map printed on cloth, a "blood chit," and some Korean money.

The twentieth of January was a day he wasn't soon to forget. Tiger Squadron followed its usual procedure, flying northward till the Taedong River was crossed, then splitting up into two-plane elements. The day was cold and partially cloudy, but visibility was good above ten or twelve thousand feet.

Kirk and his wingman climbed to 40,000 and headed toward the Yalu. Two or three miles to their left they could see another pair of fighters from the squadron. The morning sun was on their right.

Kirk watched like a hawk—up, down, and to the sides— even behind him. MIG's, he had found, were likely to appear when and where you least expected them. This time was no exception.

French suddenly broke radio silence. "Bogies!" he said sharply. "Three o'clock high—diving out o' the sun. Duck, Kayo, an' toggle your wing tanks!"

Kirk pulled the lever that cut loose the tanks, rammed the throttle forward, and hauled back on the stick. As he shot aloft, he saw the MIG flash downward just behind him. Here, he thought, was a chance to get on the enemy's tail. He pulled the Sabre over and down in a screaming dive, trying his hardest to come within firing range. The MIG was right in his sights but still too far away.

Just then things that looked like golf balls began zipping past the canopy. They were 37-millimeter cannon shells. A second MIG was right behind him! Kirk swerved left as sharply as he dared and saw the attacker turn with him. In desperation, he banked to the right, knowing as he did so that it was hopeless. But at that instant there was a muffled blast astern of him, and when he looked back, he saw the whole enemy jet explode. A wing flew off, and the fiery mass fell earthward. In horrified fascination he waited to see the pilot bail out. But the canopy never opened.

Evan French's calm voice came through the headphones. "You all right, Kayo? I was lucky to be where I could hit him before he nailed you. That was the old decoy trick. Watch it, next time."

"Gosh, Captain," Kirk stammered. "Thanks—for everything!"

The decoy plane had vanished during the brief battle, and though they kept on patrolling till their fuel was low, they saw no more MIG's that day.

Blue Flight celebrated the captain's confirmed kill that night in the crowded shack that did duty as an Officers' Club. When they had toasted him in beer and cokes, according to their taste, French broke the news that he had completed his quota of missions.

"There's nobody I'd rather fly with than you boys," he said. "It would be fun to stick around for a few more. But I've seen pilots push their luck too far and lose on the last one. So I'm taking off for Japan tomorrow. Any messages for Johnson AFB?"

He winked at Kirk, and the young pilot's face reddened. His engagement was a secret shared by these close friends of his. The same batch of orders that gave Captain French his release from active duty had brought good news to First Lieutenant Yokum. He was called to Wing Headquarters next morning, given his captain's bars, and appointed to the command of Blue Flight.

Both Kirk and Ron were pleased, for they liked and respected the chunky Arkansas pilot. But Kirk was still without a wingman, and he knew he was going to miss Evan French. As it happened, his own plane was grounded that day for an overhaul, and Yokum and Ron took off without him.

He was in the hangar that afternoon overseeing the job, and when one of the mechanics showed that he didn't know the proper technique, Kirk grew restless.

"Here," he said, "let me at that thing. If you'd learned under old Claggett at Nellis, you could do it with your eyes shut."

He stripped off his uniform blouse and got into a greasy coverall. Working away happily, he looked down and saw a pair of well-shined shoes and pressed blue trousers standing beside him.

"Hi," said a pleasant New England voice at his elbow. "Is this Blue Flight's hangar?"

Kirk straightened quickly. "Gosh!" he exclaimed. "It's Lieutenant Peabody. Say—are you here to fly with us?"

Peabody nodded. "That's right. Going to fly wing on the kid pilot that's No. 1 in Blue Flight, whoever he is. And it'll be great having you for a crewman again, Owen. You always kept my plane in top shape."

Kirk looked at him to make sure he wasn't kidding. Then

a glance at his own greasy hands and smudged pants made him chuckle.

"Lieutenant," he said, "don't hold it against me, but I'm out of practice as a mechanic. This is my own jet I'm tinkering with. You see—well, I'm the kid pilot you're going to be nursing in Tiger Blue."

He got back into uniform and showed Peabody around the base. When the squadron returned, he introduced his old friend to the other two members of Blue Flight. Yokum and the Maine man were already acquainted. They had been squadron-mates the year before at Suwon, and when they started telling tall tales about those days, the down-east twang and the hill-billy drawl made a strange and wonderful combination.

Lieutenant Peabody had flown close to a hundred combat missions, but he appeared to be as eager as when Kirk had known him at Nellis. "Heck!" he told them. "I've got no wife to go home to. Fighting MIG's is as good a way to spend my time as any, and I figure I'm just getting my hand in. I'd been over here eight months before I got my first probable. Then I guess I must have found the touch. I shot down three in a week, and they sent me off to Japan for a rest. Now I'm back and ready for more. Sure would like to make ace this trip!"

Kirk's jet was in good flying shape next morning. Blue Flight took a half hour's shakedown hop before lunch to familiarize the new pilot with the nearby country. And that afternoon they loaded up with fuel, got their briefing, and headed for the Yalu.

The Sabre units they met on the way complained that there had been no Red activity whatever.

"Ho, hum!" said Kirk. "Another milk run." It was his sixteenth flight into combat territory, and he was beginning to talk like an old hand.

They passed over Sinanju at 40,000, still flying at an easy
350 knots. It was 1600 hours now, and with only an hour or
two of winter daylight left, it was unlikely that any MIG
fighters would be up. The two elements divided, roaming
along a mile or so apart.

For all his watchfulness, it was pure luck that Kirk happened to look down at the snowy hills to their rear. Half-
hidden by the background of woods and snow, he saw eight
specks shooting upward like leaves in a whirlwind. He
jammed down the radio button.

"Bogies!" he yelled. "Five o'clock low—coming up fast
—eight of 'em."

He dropped his tanks, shoved the throttle up, and banked
to the right. The MIG's were over at his left, heading
straight for Ron's plane, and the nearest one was already
shooting. He saw his friend go into a frantic climb and loop,
with cannon shells spraying past his wings. The other enemy
planes had split up their formation, leaving only the two
leading jets to follow Ron. Out of the tail of his eye he saw
one pair tangling with Captain Yokum. The others must be
headed for his wingman and himself. But the one thing he
thought of in that instant was how to save Ron.

He came out of the turn in a power dive, cutting straight
across the intervening distance at better than 700 miles an
hour. His path put him behind MacLean's attackers and a
little below them. He slammed into a climbing turn, caught
the nearest MIG in his gunsight, and squeezed off a sharp
burst of fire. The tracers flew straight up the enemy jet's tail
pipe. By amazing luck his .50-caliber slugs must have ripped
clear through the turbine and into the compressor, for a
great gush of smoke and flying metal poured from the tail
vent. Out of control, the MIG fell off on one wing, and Kirk
had to pull his nose up fast to avoid hitting the damaged
plane. He was too busy to watch it longer.

USAF
4501

Up ahead, Ron was still in trouble. The enemy jet nearest him was hanging on his tail, outmaneuvering and outclimbing the heavier Sabre at every turn. Kirk could see shell holes in the skin of the fuselage, and part of the tail surface was shot away.

In a desperate effort at evasion, Ron swerved sharply to the left, and for a second he was clear of Kirk's line of fire. The pursuing MIG turned after him, still blazing away with his cannon. Kirk, 200 yards behind, knew it was now or never. He felt suddenly cool and sure as he found the attacker in his sights. Then his guns hemstitched a row of hits right along the side of the jet from nose to tail.

There was no question about that one. The MIG came apart in the air with an explosion that shook Kirk's plane.

The whole fight had taken perhaps twenty seconds, and there had been no time for talk. Now, as he looked around, Kirk saw that the rest of the MIG pack had broken off action and headed north, with Yokum still in hot pursuit.

"Number two to Blue one," came Peabody's calm voice. "Nice shooting, Kayo. Let's get our boy home. How's she handle, Ron?"

"Still in one piece," Ron replied with a catch in his voice. "Thank the Lord these birds are built tough. I think I can make it, but you'd better stick with me."

Kirk pushed the radio button. "Blue one to captain," he said. "Do you read me? We're on our way. Number three's been damaged. Over."

"I read you clear," Yokum's voice came back. "Roger. Be with you shortly. Over."

He overtook the rest of the flight before they landed at Kimpo, for they had cruised slowly, nursing the wounded jet. After the action Kirk felt let down. His knees shook a little when he climbed down from his plane. One by one the others came over and shook his hand.

"You are now officially a tiger," said Lieutenant Peabody solemnly. "And how! Two confirmed. I saw the pilot of that first one bail out. Quite a day's work."

"Blue Flight's proud of you," Yokum told him. "Afraid I wasn't a very good wingman, but both of us old tigers had our hands full. Then when the little devils turned tail, I never did catch 'em."

Ron didn't say much, but he put his gratitude into his handshake. He knew how close he had been to death.

When Kirk was alone that night, he thought back over the battle and knew he had only done what he had to do. He felt no qualms over knocking out the two jets. It was Ron's life or theirs, and they had been the aggressors. Deep inside he had a glow of pride and satisfaction.

Next day he found two red stars posted after his name on the briefing-room board, and envious pilots trooped around him asking about the fight. He was suddenly a hero, and it embarrassed him. Then Ron arrived with a brush and a can of red paint.

"If you want any help, Kayo," he said with a grin, "I can draw a pretty fair star."

He proved it in the next few minutes as he painted two small red stars just below the cockpit canopy of Kirk's Sabre. "Too bad they won't let us put names on the planes," he said. "You could call this one 'Kayo Tiger'!"

17

Through the month of February they flew three or four missions a week. Usually they saw MIG formations, and several times they succeeded in getting close enough for a hassle. However, the Chinese pilots appeared to have grown cautious again. They rarely maneuvered more than ten miles below the Yalu, and the moment a serious fight threatened, they fled back to their fields at Antung or Tapao.

A thaw came in early March. The hard crust of snow that had covered the hills melted in the sun, and the ice broke in the rivers. Sometimes, when they were flying at lower altitudes, the members of Blue Flight saw farmers working knee-deep in the flooded rice paddies.

"Brrrr!" Kirk shivered. "I bet that water's cold!"

Winter wasn't over, but as the days went by and the sun climbed higher in the sky, there were fewer snowfalls, fewer freezing nights. They felt that spring was really on the way.

The lack of real combat was becoming irksome to the pilots. Their squadron commander knew the signs and urged them to be patient.

"Don't worry," he said. "I've been here long enough to know something about these Red fliers. When the sap starts to run, they get cocky and come out to fight. You may find some pretty good pilots among them, too. So keep on your toes."

On the seventeenth of March—St. Patrick's Day—Kirk flew his fortieth mission. He was two or three ahead of Ron, whose Sabre had been laid up for repairs for a week. There was an overcast that morning, but it cleared by 1400, and their flight, along with several others, prepared to take off.

Kirk had a strange hunch about this mission. Something important was going to happen, he thought, as he went through the cockpit check.

They headed northward above the familiar terrain, passed the forward outposts of the UN lines, and saw American bombers working over the Chinese troop concentrations beyond the Taedong. When they were some fifty miles south of the Yalu, a drawling Texas voice came in faintly over the radio.

"This is Houn'-dawg leader," it said. "We're engagin' eight MIG's ten miles south o' Suiho Dam at angels thirty-five. If y'all want some action, come on in."

Kirk knew that "Hound-dog" was a flight from another squadron based at Suwon. The hassle probably wouldn't last long, but it was worth a try.

"Blue skipper to flight," Yokum called. "Climb to 35,000 and let's go. Suiho Dam's straight ahead. Over."

Kirk pushed the throttle forward, and the jet boomed up in a long, fast climb. Four minutes later he saw the darting flecks of light on metal that meant fighter planes in action. "Better clean 'em up," Yokum told the flight and immediately jettisoned his own tanks.

There were a lot of planes ahead. The eight MIG's must have been joined by others, and at least four elements of Sabres were giving them battle. Blue Flight closed fast, heading straight for the melee.

Kirk took a last look upward and backward before he got too near. It was lucky he did. Three Red jets had circled behind them and were diving out of the sun.

"Bogies!" he yelled. "Seven o'clock high and coming down fast!"

The flight split outward, Kirk and Peabody swerving to the right, Ron and Yokum to the left. Kirk saw the nearest MIG plunge past his flank and did a quick wing-over to dive after it. He expected evasive action from the MIG pilot and was prepared to maneuver with him. But to his surprise the enemy jet continued its dive. The altimeter showed 30,-000, then 25,000. Kirk didn't cut his power. He was gaining—another few seconds and he thought he would be within long shooting range.

He glanced back, and the sky was empty. Peabody must have decided he could handle this single MIG alone, or else the wingman was engaged in a hassle of his own.

They were below 20,000 feet now. Kirk had the other jet in his gunsight, but it was still just a bit too far. He fired a short burst to make sure and saw the tracers miss their target.

He was so intent on his quarry that he didn't notice the puffs of smoke below until it was too late. There was a slamming explosion so close to his plane that it nearly bounced the stick out of his hand. Then came another even nearer, and shell fragments struck some part of the jet.

As he tried to pull out of the dive, a light flashed on the panel in front of him giving warning that the hydraulic system was out of order. He made an effort to turn to the left and got the Sabre part way around when he realized his rudder pedals were no longer working.

Spinning crazily for a moment, the jet steadied itself on a southerly course and began to lose altitude. The altimeter showed 15,000 feet. He still had full power on, and he decided to leave it so until he got out of range of the anti-aircraft battery that was shooting at him. As he boomed along, the nose of the plane suddenly jerked upward. He put both hands and both feet against the stick and pushed, but it was frozen. The Sabre pulled up to the stall point, and the nose dropped again.

Over and over it happened, while the sweat streamed down Kirk's face inside the helmet. His progress was a series of plunges, climbs, and stalls, and he was as powerless to do anything about it as if he had been riding a giant roller coaster. All he could do was hang on and pray.

The thing went on and on. At each downward skid he was losing a little altitude. The rugged hills were getting too close for comfort. He realized that he was going to have to bail out before much longer. Collecting his faculties, he tried to figure his position. When the fight started, he had been possibly fifteen miles below the Yalu. His best guess was that he had been hit another ten miles south of that point, and his porpoising flight had carried him perhaps a hundred miles to the southeast—still a long way inside the enemy lines. He was too far inland to see the Bay of West Korea, and if he had, he knew he couldn't turn the plane in that direction. On both sides of him and in the distance ahead were mountains higher than he was.

When the altimeter read 3,000 feet, he pushed the radio button, not knowing whether he could be heard or not.

"May Day!" he called. "This is Tiger Blue one calling all friendlies. Bailing out somewhere about east of Pyongyang. If you hear me, send a chopper."

He thought back to the day at Williams when he had ridden the "boom bucket." He had wondered then if he would ever have to fire the ejection seat in actual flight. Well—this was it. He went over the procedure quickly in his mind. If it didn't work—but it had to or he was done for.

He settled his feet in the stirrups, felt for the ejection triggers on the right-hand armrest, and found them. Waiting till the plane was in comparatively level flight, he pulled the first one. The canopy flew off with a *whoosh*. Now the one that would fire the seat.

"Dear God," he muttered between his teeth, "make it work."

As he pressed the trigger, he was hurled up and out with stunning force. But his numb mind remembered the lessons learned in ground school. "Get rid of the seat first," it told him, and with fumbling fingers he released the catch that let the heavy ejection seat fall clear.

He was well behind the plane now. The D-ring for the parachute rip-cord was on the left side of the harness. He groped for it, found it, and pulled hard. When the chute opened and he recovered his breath after the jerk, he prayed again—this time a silent prayer of thankfulness.

The gyrating motion stopped, and he was dropping gently earthward, the chute a white billow above him. He tossed away his helmet and oxygen mask. From the fact that the sun was on his right, he knew he was facing southeastward—the same direction in which his plane had been headed. But the poor old "Kayo Tiger" was no longer in sight. Somewhere off there in the distance it must have rammed into a rocky hilltop.

Looking down, he found the earth coming near. He might be a thousand feet above sea level, but the wooded ground was much closer than that. There were barren, rocky slopes beyond the woods, but at the rate he was drifting he wasn't going to reach them. He was going to come down among trees. All he could hope for was that he might fall between them.

The bare limbs of the oaks were very near now. He could

see every twig and tattered brown leaf. Awkwardly he hauled at the chute cords, trying to steer himself away from the higher treetops. Then, with a crackle of small branches he came down. At the last second he tried to shield his face with his arms, and his left forearm was struck by the backlash of a bending limb. He stopped with a jarring bump and found himself straddling a crotch of the tree, thirty feet from the ground.

For a few heartbeats he clung there bruised and aching but glad to be alive. Then he took stock of the situation. The chute would surely betray his presence if it was seen by passing Chinese or North Koreans. But it was so hopelessly tangled in the branches he doubted if he could clear it. Also there was always a chance that a UN plane might spot the white patch from the air and so have a clue to his whereabouts.

The first thing he must do, he decided, was to climb down and find a hiding place. He worked himself around to try to grasp the trunk of the tree, and it was then he discovered that his left arm was broken between the wrist and the elbow. He had noticed the pain of the blow but thought little of it. Now, when he tried to grasp the tree, he found his left hand useless. There was a nasty, throbbing ache in the arm, too, that made him feel faint.

Gritting his teeth, Kirk got the knife out of his right jacket pocket and started cutting away the parachute harness. That gave him an idea. He pulled in as many of the nylon cords as he could and cut them off. They were small but very strong, and when he finished, he had some sixty feet in all. Knotting them together end to end was the most difficult task. Finally, using his teeth and one hand, he managed it.

Now for the descent. He slung his improvised rope over the tree crotch with the two ends hanging to the ground.

Then, holding onto the limb with his right arm, he eased his legs down till he could get them part way around the tree trunk. Slowly he slid downward, hanging onto the rope as best he could with one hand. At last, panting from the strain, he felt his feet touch the earth. In spite of his aching arm, that sense of being on solid ground was wonderfully sweet.

He pulled the rope down, coiled it, and thrust it into his pocket. Then he looked about him. He couldn't stay here. He had to move—to get as far away as he could and as fast as he could. The chances were strong that somebody had seen the falling parachute and was already hurrying to the spot. He ought to wait long enough to do something about the broken arm but that would have to come later.

First he discarded the dead weight of the folded rubber boat. That was one part of his evasion equipment he would hardly need. It was carried for ditching in the sea, and he knew he was a long way from the sea. He kicked the yellow dinghy under a pile of brush and started hiking through the woods, bearing toward the south. It was after 1800 by his wrist watch, and with a low bank of clouds covering the sun it was already growing dusk.

There was no path. The going was rough, and he stumbled often among fallen trees, rocks, and briars. The grinding pain in his arm was a constant misery. He went downhill for half a mile, then crossed a swampy gully, and started up a steeper slope on the other side.

Several times he saw small animals—rabbits, he thought —dashing away through the thickets. Once a deer walked gracefully across in front of him. It was hard to see his way as the darkness deepened, and he was tired, sweating from the exertion of climbing in his heavy flight jacket.

Near the top of the ridge he stopped to rest a moment and listen. The evening was still. A night bird squawked once or twice in the trees above him, and from somewhere far off to the west he heard the wailing hoot of a locomotive.

Over at his left there was a jumbled pile of ledges and boulders half-screened by brush. At the base of the pile was a small opening that looked like a cave in the dim light. He made his way to it and found a cranny under an overhanging rock that would at least give him some shelter. The bottom was fairly level. He kicked together a heap of dead leaves and spread them inside, then crouched in the entrance of the crevice and started taking off his jacket.

It wasn't easy, for the pain in his left arm made him wince at every movement. When he got it off, he undid the lacing and rolled up the sleeve of the G-suit. His forearm was swollen and appeared slightly bent, but there was no bleeding. The break was about halfway up toward the elbow.

He dug out his first-aid kit and found a small roll of bandage. But before he tried to put it on, he thought the fracture should be supported by a splint. Again he got to his feet, and in the increasing darkness he hunted around till he found a finger-thick sapling. With his knife he cut off two pieces, each about a foot long. They were pretty poor splints, but they would have to do for now.

Getting them in place on either side of the arm and holding them there while he attempted to apply a tight bandage was awkward and took a lot of time. It was almost pitch-dark when he finished the makeshift job. Panting and exhausted, he lay back on the bed of dry leaves and closed his eyes.

Kirk woke with a start an hour or two later. Moonlight was shining in his eyes, and it had grown much colder. He got out his little flashlight and checked his watch. The time was close to 2300. He knew he ought to be up and traveling.

As he reached for the flight jacket his fingers came in contact with something in a fold of the fleece lining—something cold and smooth and alive. He jerked his hand away and sprang to his feet, hitting the top of his head against the low stone roof. For a moment he swayed there, staggered by the blow. Then, as his brain cleared, he picked up the jacket by the collar and shook it. A three-foot snake tumbled out and went slithering away in the dark. It had crawled into the cave with him to get warm.

The boy didn't wait to find out if there were any more of them around. He pulled the jacket over his shoulders and set off across the ridge, still trying to hold a southerly course. Soon he was moving downhill again. The trees seemed thicker, the ground rougher and more strewn with obstacles than ever. He fell several times but managed to twist so that he avoided hitting the broken arm. The moon was very close to setting now, and it was harder for him to see where he was going. Worst of all, he felt lightheaded. Perhaps the agony of binding up his arm had made him feverish.

Finally he fell again and stayed where he lay. He was in a kind of sheltered thicket—a good enough hiding place for the moment, he thought. It was too much of an effort to get out the flashlight, so he didn't know what time it was or how far he had come. Once more he was almost instantly asleep.

18

Gray dawn and a chirping of birds woke him. He lay there a little while listening, hating to move his sore muscles. Then he realized that though the fever seemed to be gone, his mouth was as dry as cotton. Somehow he had to find water. Stiffly he got to his feet and looked about him. The early daylight showed only a dismal wilderness of rocks and trees, but the general slope of the terrain was southward. That was the way he felt he must go and keep on going. No matter how far he had to travel, that was where the front lines lay.

Oddly, he realized, the arm in its crude splints and bandages was less painful this morning. The feeling in it had subsided to a dull, steady ache. He wished now that he had been able to salvage a little of the parachute to make a sling. As it was, he had to hook his left thumb into his belt to keep the arm from dangling.

Twenty minutes later he came to a small spring that bubbled out among the rocks and ran off in a tiny rivulet. No need to use chlorination tablets, he thought. Clear, cold spring water should be safe. He drank deep and filled his plastic water bag, then got out his little cloth map and tried to figure where he was. During his wild flight in the damaged plane he should have been watching for landmarks, but his eyes had been glued to the altimeter most of the time. Vaguely he recalled passing above a big river flanked by a highway. That, he thought, must have been the Nan-gang, somewhere well to the east of Pyongyang. Shortly after, he remembered, there had been a mile-high mountain off to his right. Possibly that was Taegak-san. Then there was a valley with a road running down it, and about that time he had decided to bail out. If all his guesses were correct, he had landed in the hills somewhere between the Yesong and the Imjin Rivers. He looked doubtfully at the spot on the map. It was some forty miles northwest of Chorwon and Sang-nyong, which were on the front line. That was as the crow flies. By the river valleys it might be seventy miles or more.

He was hungry, but he didn't touch his C-rations yet. He knew that if he was lucky enough to avoid capture he had a lot of traveling ahead.

Every now and then he stopped to listen, for moving in the daytime was dangerous. On the steep hillside he was less likely to find farms or villages, so he kept on along the east slope of the ridge, bearing steadily southward. It was full daylight now, and he had been walking at least an hour. Three miles—four miles—he didn't know. But it was time to look around for a place to hide. At that moment he heard a sound of voices in the distance.

Kirk saw a brush thicket fifty feet up the hill, and he ran for it clumsily, falling once and jolting his fractured arm. The pain made him feel faint, and he almost blacked out. The sweat poured from his face. But he crawled into the middle of the thicket and lay still.

The voices were coming nearer. They came in irregular snatches, a few words spoken in high Korean singsong, then an interval of silence. At last he saw a movement among the trees. Two young farmers were climbing the hillside, following a rough path not more than thirty yards from where he lay. They were dressed in coarse blue cotton smocks and trousers and carried axes on their shoulders. Evidently they were on their way to cut firewood.

Kirk waited till they were well up the hill and he could hear the sound of distant chopping. Then he crept out of the brush and moved cautiously southward. When he crossed the path, he could look down and see a cluster of three or four mud houses and some fields at the foot of the slope. From now on he must go more carefully, for he was no longer in the wilderness.

After another mile or so he decided to hole up and wait till evening. There was a rocky ledge up at his right, and under it he saw the mouth of another small cave. It had begun to rain, and he was glad to get under shelter. Huddled there behind the dripping water that fell from the front of the ledge, he thought about his plight and how to get out of it. There was some temptation to feel sorry for himself, but he resisted it. He was a fighter pilot—a tiger—and supposed to be able to take care of himself.

Only two things really worried him. One was his arm, which now ached more than ever and felt swollen and hot. The other was food. It had been nearly twenty-four hours since he had eaten, and there was a constant, gnawing hunger in his stomach. Somehow he had to get food in order to keep up his strength. He tried to remember all he had learned about the subject in survival classes. But very little of his knowledge seemed to apply here. "You can eat anything a monkey eats" was one of the facts he had been taught. He grinned. In North Korea monkeys were about as plentiful as giraffes. Another lesson had covered fruits and berries. March wasn't the season for them.

As the day wore on, he did find something he could put in his mouth, though he wasn't sure he got any nourishment. There were some young fiddlehead ferns sprouting just outside his cave, and he chewed and swallowed half a dozen of them. Then he tried acorns. The bitter meat made him gag a little, and he gave up after the first two or three. Perhaps, he thought, he could catch a fish. Back home he knew they wouldn't bite well in the rain, but Korean fish might be different. He took out the hook and line from his E & E kit and succeeded in tieing the hook on after half an hour's one-handed work. Now all he had to find was a river and some bait.

Lack of food hadn't weakened him noticeably as yet. About 1600 in the afternoon he decided it was safe to travel again, for the drizzle made it unlikely that he would meet anyone. Down on his left, to the east of the ridge, the valley had widened out now. He saw several small villages at a distance, and then he caught a glint of water. There was a river there, or at least a fair-sized stream, winding through the fields.

After another mile or two he saw that a bend in the stream brought it close to the woods at the foot of the hill. He began working his way cautiously down in that direction. Soon he was on the bank. The water was muddy and only about ten yards across. It was flowing quite fast, however, and right below him there was an eddy at a bend, where he thought there might be fish. With his knife he dug into the earth and found a worm which he finally managed to get on the hook.

Lying on his stomach, half-concealed by branches, he fished for the better part of an hour. There were no bites. He grew more and more discouraged each time he pulled out the hook to see if his bait was still on. He tried different sized pebbles as sinkers but still with no success.

"Dear God," he prayed, "please let me catch just one fish, even a little one."

The rain stopped shortly after that, and a ray of late sunshine fell slantwise on the water. At the same moment Kirk felt a nibble, then a tug on his line. Breathlessly he gave a yank to set the hook, then hauled in. There was an eight-inch fish on the end of the line. It looked like a trout, but he didn't care what it was just then. He got it on shore, pulled out the hook, and stared hungrily at his catch.

He was sure now, surer than he had ever been before, that Heaven had heard his prayer.

There was no dry wood for a fire, and he would have been afraid to light one in any case. Raw fish wasn't bad. Millions of Japanese ate it every day and thrived on it. Kirk shut his eyes and bit off the tail. Then he wolfed down the rest of the fish, bones and all.

He baited the hook again, and before dark he had caught two more small trout. One he ate. The other he wrapped in a handkerchief and put in his jacket pocket, hoping it would keep till morning. His stomach still had a few knots in it, but he felt somewhat better as he started hiking once more.

Kirk followed the bank of the stream. It must flow into a larger river somewhere, and he decided to reach that river. Now the stream had swung eastward, and there were more farms and villages along its course. He skirted them, climbing up into the woods where he had to. About five miles below his fishing hole he saw a village on the opposite bank and went up the hill again. It was quite dark now, and he had to feel his way among the trees. Suddenly a sound made him stop.

He listened intently, and the sound continued. It was the chugging clatter of truck engines, and it was coming from directly in front of him, over the crest of the hill. He went forward as silently as he could. The trees thinned out at the top of the rise. When he reached it, he found himself on a high bluff looking down into a valley. He could make out a wide stretch of river, and on the west side of it, the side nearest him, a string of trucks was moving slowly southward. Their lights were hooded, but in front of each there was a faint glow on the road.

The boy's heart pounded with excitement. He was sure now that he had reached the Imjin. If his memory of the terrain was right, the highway crossed the river just at that point and cut south a few miles to the big town of Inchon. Sure enough, as he watched, the trucks bore to their left, rumbling across a bridge.

Luckily he had the best part of the night ahead. He should be able to get safely past the city before dawn caught him. He followed the steep slope of the bluff, clinging to limbs and saplings with his good hand to keep from sliding down. Soon he was well below the highway bridge, and off in the distance on his left he could see the dim lights of Inchon.

There were barges and what looked like houseboats tied up along the riverbank, so he stuck to the brush-covered bluff. The river curved eastward away from him there, but he knew it would come back. At his feet now was a mile-wide area of bottom land with small farmhouses visible here and there.

He was hungry again, and the idea kept going through his head that some of the farmers might be friendly. Still, he didn't dare risk going to one of the houses and asking for food. He was too close to the supply route. Chinese soldiers could easily be quartered there.

About 0200 in the morning, still hiking slowly southward, he came to another smaller stream that ran into the Imjin from the west. A narrow footbridge, suspended by ropes, was the only way across. He rested awhile and watched the houses on the other side. There was no sign of life over there. Finally he tiptoed out on the swaying planks and crossed without too much noise.

Suddenly a dog began to bark in a mud hut to his right. He held his breath and hurried on as quietly as he could. He was on some kind of road or footpath. As soon as he had made a hundred yards, he started to run and kept it up till he was winded. The dog, meantime, had stopped yapping.

There was a small, dark shanty close to the path. It had no windows, and Kirk thought it must be a tool shed or storehouse. Very quietly he approached and put his ear against the low, rickety door. If anyone had been inside, he was sure he would have heard the breathing. After a moment's hesitation he lifted the crude wooden latch, and the door creaked open. He pulled out his .45 and had it in his hand as he slipped inside. Then, when there was no sound, he holstered the pistol and flicked the beam of his flashlight around the interior.

A big gray rat jumped from a corner and scurried out.

Then Kirk saw what the animal had been eating. Rice! There was a big bag of it there on a pole platform, and the rat had gnawed a hole in one corner.

Kirk had a bandanna in his coverall pocket. Quickly he poured three or four pounds of the grain into the handkerchief and pulled the corners together, knotting them with his teeth. He pulled the door shut behind him and hurried on along the path, jubilant over his find.

Within half a mile he was out of the bottom land and skirting the bluff once more. Then weariness began to rack him. The pain in his arm grew worse, and the ground was slippery on the hillside after the rain. Sometime before dawn he crawled under the boughs of a bushy pine tree and stretched himself on the bed of pine needles to rest.

Again the noise of birds woke him before daylight. He wasn't as hungry as he had expected. Perhaps his stomach had shrunk, he thought. With no way to cook the rice, he ate some of it raw, grinding the brown kernels between his teeth. Washed down with water, it wasn't bad. His appetite rebelled, however, at the fish he had saved. The moment he unwrapped it he knew from its rank odor that it had spoiled. He carried it some distance off and threw it as far as he could.

From his couch under the pine he was out of sight of the river. But as the morning wore on, he could catch the sound of motor traffic on the military road a mile away on the opposite shore. He wondered how near he was to the front now. Not more than twenty miles in a direct line, he was sure. Twice that afternoon the noise of trucks stopped, and there was a roar of bombers coming over. He heard the heavy thud of bomb hits in the valley and the rattle of machine-gun and antiaircraft fire.

The first time it happened he hurried to get out his little mirror and try to signal the friendly planes. But the trees

overhead interfered. By the time he reached an open space
the bombers had left the area, and he wasn't sure he remembered enough Morse to flash a message they could read. At
least he knew the three-short, three-long, three-short code
for SOS. When the B-26's returned an hour later, he signaled over and over, but apparently nobody saw the flashes.

That evening he chewed some more rice and drank all but
a cupful of his water. As a special treat he gave himself part
of the C-rations for dessert.

He knew he was approaching the toughest part of his
journey. He remembered from flying over the territory that
the big military highway from the north crossed the twisting
river three or four times in the next few miles. When he
looked at his map, it confirmed the fact. And, in addition,
the woods gave way to open ground along the banks a little
way below his present position.

After it grew dark he started again. Soon he had to come
down into the flatlands and work his way past more farms.
There were two villages as well, but he took the long way
around and avoided them. The detours added miles to his
journey, but as long as he could, he must keep away from
habitations.

Finally the bank grew steeper once more, and there were
woods to hide him. Right across the river was the big road,
clinging to the opposite side of the gorge, and the Imjin ran
deep and fast between. If he had a boat, he thought, he
could make five miles an hour drifting with that current.
About midnight he came to the end of the gorge. The Imjin
made a big bend to the northwest right across his path, and
he descended toward it uncertainly.

There were no farmhouses in sight, though he did cross
a rutted cart road near the river. Then he was among clumps
of bushes and tall reeds, close to the dark, gleaming water.
He took another step and sank in muck up to his ankle.

Trying hastily to back away from the wet spot, his heel
struck something that rang metallically, and he sat down on
a large, hard object.

Kirk felt of it with his right hand. The shape was familiar
—a sheet-iron oil drum like the ones used by truck and
tank units. He could tell by the sound when he patted it that
it was empty. Perhaps he was feverish. He sometimes wondered afterward if it was a kind of delirium that made him
decide to do the thing he did. But suddenly what seemed a
great and brilliant idea flashed into his head.

19

There was a circular opening about an inch and a half
across in one end of the drum. Kirk sniffed at it and caught
a faint odor of gasoline. In a moment he was hurrrying back
to the edge of the woods. He fumbled around till he found
a piece of dead limb a little smaller than his wrist. Then,
squatting on the ground, he held the stick tight between his
knees and whittled one end down to a tapering roundness.
Next he cut deep notches in the wood six inches from the
tapered end.

Carrying it back to the marshy spot where the oil barrel
lay, he jammed the peg into the bunghole as hard as it would
go. And with a well-aimed kick he broke the stick off at the
notches. Still filled with his great plan, he tugged and
strained at the drum till it pulled free of the mud. It was
easy then to roll it toward the river. At a dry spot a few
feet from the water he wrapped several lengths of his chute
cord around the barrel close to its upper rim and made fast
a foot-long loop of cord to the tightly tied strands.

Only when he had rolled the old drum into a shallow

place in the edge of the river did he begin to think soberly about his project. It was the cold water lapping about his legs that did it. He realized that if he floated downstream holding onto the barrel he would have to leave some of his warm clothing behind. The flight jacket and boots, for instance, would grow waterlogged and sink him. And his precious rice! Submersion in the Imjin would certainly do it no good.

He opened the bandanna bundle and spent the next half hour eating as much raw rice as he could hold. When he finished, it was somewhere in the neighborhood of 0100 hours, though he didn't dare flash the light to see his watch. He stuffed the pockets of his coveralls with the things he might need most and threw everything else into the bushes. He still thought the river offered his best chance of escape.

Resolutely he stepped out into the icy water pushing the barrel ahead of him. It floated buoyantly enough, and when he got beyond his depth, he looped the cord around his right wrist and held on, kicking with his feet. In spite of the wool socks, his toes were soon numb. Fortunately so was his broken arm. He kept on kicking until the main current caught the oil drum and began spinning him down the river.

It was here that the Imjin started a series of great looping oxbows, each a mile or two across. Watching the stars, Kirk could tell when the river swung south again, then east, northeast, and south in one giant hairpin turn after another. Except for the slow pace, he thought in his delirium, it must be something like the famous road-race courses in Europe. His mind wandered dizzily, and he imagined for a moment that he was behind the wheel of the Owen Special, skidding the turns at Le Mans.

When he had been in the river two or three hours, nothing seemed real to him any more. Perhaps he slept a little. He never knew. But shortly before daylight he was jerked back to reality in a hurry. A searchlight from the bank fell on the bobbing barrel and glared in his eyes. He drew a deep breath and ducked under water, still holding the cord. Coming up for air, he heard a shot, then another, and one of the rifle bullets ricocheted off the top of the drum with a clang and a whine. There was laughter on the shore, and the light was turned off.

Scared and shaken, Kirk hung on. For some time he must have been drifting within fifty yards of the swarming troops on the highway. Now he saw a bridge looming ahead and expected to hear more shots at any instant. Once more he filled his lungs with air and swam under water. The bridge was right above him when he stuck his head above the surface, and the rumble of trucks was like thunder in his ears.

Alternately breathing and hiding under the barrel, Kirk let the current take him another half mile before he dared float with his face out of water. The chill had gone deep into his bones. He had no feeling in his hands or feet. And dawn would be coming soon. Somehow or other he had to reach shore and get the circulation going in his limbs again. He began kicking feebly, trying to steer the steel drum to the left.

The road had crossed the river and was on the west bank now, close to the water. He could hear Chinese sentries calling to each other and see small campfires burning over there. But as he fought his way nearer to the eastern shore, he got a rude shock. Black cliffs rose almost vertically out of the river on that side. There was no beach, no foothold. And the current was running faster now. To his horror he realized that he was in one of the canyons of the Imjin.

Once, from far above in his jet, he had looked down on this place. He remembered the rushing white water, the narrow channel, and the rock-strewn river bed. That had been one thing he forgot when he launched the barrel. Now it was too late. There was nothing he could do but hang on and try to stay alive.

Kirk's mind was very clear now. He weighed his chances coolly and knew how slim they were. The rapids were not far off. He could hear their low roar, ominous and growing louder. He was moving, he thought, at least ten miles an hour.

Quietly the boy prayed for strength and courage to meet what was coming, and once more he felt at peace with himself. He had done his best.

The rapids came suddenly, buffeting him crazily, tossing the barrel from side to side and turning it end for end. He was jerked along by the cord around his wrist. Much of the time he was under water, but he gulped air when he could. He had managed to tuck the hand of his broken left arm into the front of his coverall before the white water came, and he hoped it was still there, though he could feel nothing.

Without warning, then, he was among the rocks. A heavy blow on his right side knocked the breath out of him. Another smashed at his knees. Then he was rolled under, striking the back of his head on a hidden boulder. That was when he blacked out.

*　　　*　　　*

Two or three miles south of the town of Sangnyong a patrol of infantrymen guarded the river. Batteries of artillery in the hills above covered them well, and the enemy had been fairly quiet of late. Still they watched alertly. They were short men, dark and sturdy, part of a small tough force of Greek soldiers fighting for the United Nations and the cause of freedom.

It was March 20 and a fine spring morning. Better weather had come at last. Perhaps there would be fighting again soon.

"Look," said one of the soldiers in his native tongue. "Something comes floating close to shore."

The Greek lieutenant lifted his field glasses. "Only an oil barrel," he replied. "In a moment it will lodge on that sand bar. But be careful. It might hold explosives—an enemy trick to blow us up."

The soldier saw the object come to rest in shallow water and went forward cautiously for a closer look. Suddenly he waved his arm and shouted.

"A man!" he called. "A drowned man fastened to it by a cord!"

The lieutenant and two others hurried to the spot. They waded out to the barrel and saw the pale, bloody face of a young man turned upward to the sunshine. The officer bent close for a moment, then straightened up. "He is not drowned," he said. "The breath of life is in him. Quickly— get to the radio and call for a truck. Perhaps this young pilot can be saved."

"He is one of ours?" asked a soldier.

"Yes. On his wrist is a small silver chain with a tag. He
is one of those who fly the very fast jets."

*   *   *

Kirk regained consciousness momentarily, roused by the
rough jolting of the truck. He looked about him hazily.
There were two soldiers with rifles, and he was sure at first
they were Chinese. Then one of them looked down at him
and smiled. It was a kindly smile, and Kirk drifted off again
satisfied that he wasn't a prisoner.

The next thing he knew he was being lifted out of a helicopter on a stretcher and carried to an ambulance. He
thought he must be dreaming again, for he was looking up
into the brown, grinning face of Corny Jones.

"Doggone if it ain't Kayo!" the once familiar voice rum-
bled.

" 'Scuse me, sir—Mr. Owen. Didn't notice them lieutenant's bars at first. Gotta git you to the hospital quick
now, and I'm jes' the boy kin do it."

Kirk must have passed out again right after that. When
he came back to reality, he was in a cool white bed in a
spotlessly clean ward. With his eyes still closed he heard a
strange voice speaking. ". . . amazing vitality. More than
half drowned and covered with bruises from head to foot.
His left arm was badly broken, too—both the ulna and
radius. That must have happened earlier, though, for he had
it bandaged and splinted after a fashion. The real wonder is
he didn't die of exposure. Must have been in that cold water
a good many hours."

There were other voices then that made Kirk open his
eyes. Major Groome and Ron MacLean were talking to the
doctor.

"The main thing," said the Squadron Commander, "is
that you think he'll pull through. This boy's a tiger—and I

mean a *tiger*. Whether he ever flies again or not, he deserves to live."

"Amen to that, sir," Ron put in. "He saved my life once—twice if you count both those MIG's—and he's the best friend I ever had."

"Well," the medical officer replied, "barring some sort of trouble we haven't found yet, I think I can promise you he'll be all right. We'll keep him here at Seoul till he's strong enough, then send him back to Tokyo to get well."

Kirk couldn't turn his head, but he managed to speak. "Hi, Ron," he murmured weakly. "Good to see you, Major. And don't worry. I'll make it."

He slept after they were gone and woke feeling stronger. But the nurse told him he would be staying there, in the Suwon Base Hospital, for at least two more weeks.

Gradually the pain and weakness wore off. With his arm in a cast he was allowed to get up and walk around a little. It was close to the end of his stay, a day or two before he was to fly to Tokyo on convalescent leave, when a wheel chair rolled slowly up to his bedside. The pale, thin young man who occupied it smiled. He was wearing a hospital robe; a blanket was wrapped around his legs; and his head, from the eyebrows up, was covered by a tight skullcap bandage.

"Lieutenant Owen?" said the visitor. "I heard the nurse talking about you and wondered if you weren't someone I knew. My name's Castleman."

Kirk sat upright. "Grant Castleman!" he shouted. "Haven't seen you since A & E School! What put you in here, guy?"

"Same thing you got—Chinese flak. Only I was lucky and didn't have to swim home. After I got transferred from Sheppard, I was shifted around in different parts of the Air Force and finally wound up here, flying as observer in a B-26. We were doing low-level bombing up near Chorwon when we caught it. The pilot was able to bring her back, but I never knew what hit me until I came to in the hospital."

"You must have had a bad head wound," Kirk remarked sympathetically.

"Not too bad." Castleman's mouth twisted in a grin. "I guess they'll be shipping me home pretty soon."

The blanket on his lap slipped a little, and Kirk saw the stump of his left leg, gone above the knee. Hastily the airman covered it again. He saw the consternation in Kirk's face and laughed.

"Don't look so shocked," he said. "They're going to give me a brand-new one that'll let me walk—play games—even dance! When you see me strutting around in sport clothes, you'll be jealous."

They were both silent for a moment. "I remember," Kirk said at last, "when we started at Lackland, you didn't think much of the Air Force. How do you feel about it now?"

"I'm proud," Castleman answered simply. "It's the greatest."

*   *   *

May is a lovely month in Japan. The jewel-like little gardens are at their freshest and most colorful, and the air is warm and balmy.

Kirk and Ginnie walked slowly together through such a spring morning. He was an ambulatory patient now, out of bed for three weeks past, and gaining strength every day. His left arm was still in a cast, but the bruises were gone, along with the terrible dreams that had bothered him at first. And Ginnie, he thought, was more beautiful than ever.

They sat down beside a little arching bridge under a graceful pine tree and watched the ducks swim slowly past. Ginnie squeezed his good arm.

"Do you really want to go back?" she asked. "The officers at Headquarters seem to think the fighting is about over. The truce might be signed any time now."

Kirk smiled. "Could be," he said. "But I'm a pilot, honey. The Air Force doesn't stop when a war stops. I guess I'll never be an ace now, but if they need me, I'll be there. I might still get in a few more missions. What's more, they like to have escapees and evasion cases around to tell the greenies how it's done. You forget I'm some kind of side-show character, Ginnie. I've even got medals and ribbons to prove it."

She laughed. "All right, darling, I give up. But I'm holding you to the promise you made the first time I came to the hospital. We're getting married on my next furlough, whether the fighting's over or not."

"That," he said, "is right. We'll get married by the chaplain at Johnson Air Force Base. And Ronnie's going to be my best man. Maybe some more of the Tigers can come if there's a truce. And you, Ginnie—have you picked out what you're going to wear at the wedding?"

She looked dreamily at the ducks. "Yes," she said with a little smile. "I'm going to be an Air Force wife. So I guess it will be Air Force blue."